READER REVIEWS FOR

GIRL, MISSING

"really good" Rebecca

"everything you would want in a book . . . amazing" Iris

"fantastic, an amazing page-turner"
Susan

"the best book I have ever read"
Hugh

"so good I read it twice in one day!"
Flava

"this book is the best!!!"
Brian

"the best book ever written . . . the ultimate"
Amy

"absolutely wonderful"
Maggie

"I couldn't put the book down!"
Kirsten

"you are totally gripped from beginning to end . . . brilliant stuff!"
Jacob

"a fantastic read . . . at the end of the book you want it to carry on because you grow so close to the characters"
Andrew

"full of adventure . . . had me biting my nails!"
Jennifer

All reviews taken from amazon.co.uk

Award-winning books from Sophie McKenzie

GIRL, MISSING

Winner Richard and Judy Best Kids' Books 2007 12+
Winner of the Red House Children's Book Award 2007 12+
Winner of the Manchester Children's Book Award 2008
Winner of the Bolton Children's Book Award
Winner of the Grampian Children's Book Award 2008
Winner of the John Lewis Solihull Book Award 2008
Winner of the Lewisham Children's Book Award
Winner of the 2008 Sakura Medal

SIX STEPS TO A GIRL

Winner of the Manchester Children's Book Award 2009

BLOOD TIES

Overall winner of the Red House Children's Book Award 2009
Winner of the Leeds Book Award 2009 age 11-14 category
Winner of the Spellbinding Award 2009
Winner of the Lancashire Children's Book Award 2009
Winner of the Portsmouth Book Award 2009 (Longer Novel section)
Winner of the Staffordshire Children's Book Award 2009
Winner of the Southern Schools Book Award 2010
Winner of the RED Book Award 2010
Winner of the Warwickshire Secondary Book Award 2010
Winner of the Grampian Children's Book Award 2010
Winner of the North East Teenage Book Award 2010

THE MEDUSA PROJECT: THE SET-UP

Winner of the North-East Book Award 2010
Winner of the Portsmouth Book Award 2010
Winner of the Yorkshire Coast Book Award 2010

SOPHIE McKENZIE

GIRL, MISSING

SIMON AND SCHUSTER

For my Mum, who first read me stories.
And for Joe, who read this story first.

SIMON AND SCHUSTER
First published in Great Britain in 2006 by Simon & Schuster UK Ltd
1st Floor, 222 Gray's Inn Road, London WC1X 8HB
A CBS COMPANY

A CIP catalogue record for this book is available from the British Library.

ISBN: 978-0-85707-413-3

10 8 7 9

Typeset by Palimpsest Book Production Limited,
Grangemouth, Stirlingshire

Printed and bound by CPI Group (UK) Ltd, Croydon, CR0 4YY

www.sophiemckenziebooks.com
www.simonandschuster.co.uk

PART ONE
FINDING MARTHA

1

Who am I?

Who am I?

I sat at the computer in Mum's office and stared at the essay heading. New form teachers always give you homework like that at the start of the year.

Who am I?

When I was younger it was easy. I'd just write down obvious stuff like: *I am Lauren Matthews. I have brown hair and blue eyes.*

But now we're supposed to write about what interests us. Likes and dislikes. Who we are 'inside'.

I needed a break.

I texted my friend Jam. *hw u dng w/ stpd 'who am i' thng?*

A minute later he texted back: *We are sorry to inform you that James 'Jam' Caldwell died from boredom while working on his homework earlier tonight.*

I laughed out loud. Jam always cheers me up. Some of the girls in my class tease me about him. Make out he's my boyfriend. Which is like the stupidest thing ever. Jam and I have been friends since Primary.

Who am I?

I put my head in my hands.

How can anyone work out who they are, unless they know where they come from?

And I have no idea where I come from.

I was adopted when I was three.

A minute later and Mum was calling from downstairs. 'Lauren. Tea's ready.'

I raced down, glad to get away from the essay.

I didn't get away from it for long.

'How's the homework going?' Mum asked, prodding something in a frying pan.

'Mmmn,' I mumbled.

'For goodness' sake, Lauren,' Mum sighed. 'Why can't you speak properly?'

I looked at her. Same old Mum. Short. Bony. Thin-lipped.

I look nothing like her.

I spoke very clearly and slowly. 'Who is my real mother?'

Mum froze. For a second she looked terrified. Then her face went hard like a mask. No emotion.

'I am,' she said. 'What do you mean?'

'Nothing.' I looked away, wishing I hadn't said anything.

Mum sat down, the frying pan still in her hand.

'I thought you weren't bothered about knowing,' she said.

I rolled my eyes. 'I'm not.'

Mum ladled scrambled eggs onto my plate. 'Anyway, I can't tell you. It was a closed adoption. That means neither side knows anything about the other.' She got up, replaced the frying pan on the cooker and turned back to me. Her face was all anxious now. 'Has someone said something at school?'

'No.' I bent over my eggs. Trust Mum to assume somebody else was putting ideas in my head. It would be too much for her to imagine I might have started thinking about it for myself.

'What's for tea?' Rory pelted in from the garden, his fat cheeks red from the cold air. Rory's eight and the spit of my dad. 'My little test-tube miracle,' my mum calls him. All I can say is, a lot of unpleasant things grow in test tubes.

Rory skidded to a halt at the table, then made a face. 'Scrambled eggs stink.'

'Not as much as you,' I said.

Rory picked up his fork and prodded me with it.

'Ow. Mum, he's hitting me.'

Mum glared at us both. 'Sit, Rory.' Sometimes I wonder if she thinks he's a dog. I heard her say once to a friend, 'Boys are like puppies. All they need is affection and fresh air. Girls are much harder work.'

So why choose me – a girl – in the first place? I remembered all the times when I was little that Mum talked to me about being adopted – about how they picked me out of some catalogue. It used to make me feel special. Wanted. Now it made me feel like a mail-order dress. A dress that didn't fit but that was too much trouble to send back.

'Can Jam come round later?' I asked.

'When you've done your homework – if it isn't too late,' came Mum's predictable reply.

'These eggs look like your puke,' Rory said.

Sometimes I really, really hate him.

I emailed Jam as soon as I went back upstairs.

C u l8r?

His reply came back in seconds: *ill b thr @ 7.*

I checked the time on the corner of the screen: 6.15. I was never going to finish my essay in forty-five minutes.

Who am I?

Adopted. Lost. I typed the words into the search engine box.

I'd been thinking about it a lot recently. Last week I'd even checked out some of the adoption information websites. You'd have laughed if you'd seen me: heart thumping, palms sweating, stomach screwed up into a knot.

I mean, it's not as if there's going to be some site that says: *Lauren Matthews – click here for your adoption details.*

Anyway. D'you know what I found out?

That if I wanted to know anything about my life before I was three, I needed Mum and Dad's permission.

How unbelievable is that?

My life. My identity. My past.

But their decision.

Even if I asked, there's no way Mum would say yes. Well, you've seen how she is about the subject. Gets a face on her like a smashed plate.

It would serve her right if I went ahead and did it anyway.

I clicked on the search icon.

Adopted. Lost. Nearly a million hits.

My heart thudded. I could feel my stomach clenching again.

I sat back in my chair. Enough.

I was just wasting time. Putting off the homework. I reached over to close the search. And that's when I caught sight of it: *Missing Children.com.* An international site for lost or missing children. I frowned. I mean, how do you lose a child and them not turn up? I can see how you might lose one for five minutes. Or even an hour. And I know sometimes children go missing 'cause some psycho's murdered them. But Mum's always saying that only happens like once or twice a year.

I clicked through to the homepage. It was a flickering mass of faces. Each face the size of a stamp; each stamp turning into a new face after a few seconds.

My jaw dropped. Did all these faces belong to missing children? I saw a search field. I hesitated. Then I tapped in my name. *Lauren.* I wasn't really thinking about what I was doing. Just messing about – seeing how many missing Laurens there were out there.

It turned out there were one hundred and seventy-two. Jeez. The computer was flashing at me to refine my search.

Part of me wanted to stop. But I told myself not to be stupid. The flickering faces on the screen weren't adopted children like me – with no past. They were missing kids. Kids with *only* a past.

I just wanted to see who was there.

I added my birth month to the search criteria, then watched as three Laurens appeared on the screen. One was black, missing since she was two weeks old.

One was white with blonde hair – she looked about nine or ten. Yeah – she'd only been missing five years.

I stared at the third child.

Martha Lauren Purditt
Case type: lost, injured, missing
Date of birth: March 12
Age now: 14
Birth place: Evanport, Connecticut, USA
Hair: brown *Eyes: blue*

I looked at the face above the words. A chubby, smiling little girl's face. Then at the date she'd gone missing: *September 8.*

Less than two months before I was adopted.

My heart seemed to stop beating.

The birth date was a couple of days out. And I was British, not from America like the missing girl.

So it wasn't possible.

Was it?

The question seeped like a drug through my head, turning me upside down and inside out, filling me up.

Could I be her?

2

Telling Jam

I stared at the little girl on the screen, searching her face for signs that she might be me.

'Lauren, Jam's here.' Mum's shout made me jump.

My heart raced as Jam's footsteps pounded up the stairs. I reached forward and minimised the screen. I ran to the door, just as Jam got there.

'Hi Laurenzo.' Jam smiled. His dark hair was gelled back off his face and he smelled of soap. 'Finished your homework?'

'Yeah. Er . . . no, actually.' I was hardly listening. 'I need something from downstairs.'

Jam frowned, but followed me down to the living room. Mum was sitting on the sofa watching the news on TV.

'Mum, where're our photo albums?'

She stared at me. 'End of the cupboard.' She pointed to a pair of wooden doors in the corner of the room. 'Why the sudden interest?'

I raced over and started pulling out albums, flicking through the pages. 'Where're the oldest ones of me?' I said.

Silence.

I glanced up. Mum and Jam were both looking at me as if I was mad.

'What's this about, sweetheart?' Mum's voice sounded tense.

I put down the album I was holding.

'It's for this "Who am I?" essay,' I said slowly. 'It's finished, but I thought it would be nice to put in a picture of me when I was younger, alongside one of me now. I'm only hurrying 'cause Jam's here.'

Mum's face relaxed. 'That's a good idea,' she said. 'Though I think I told you to get everything done *before* he came round. Try the green album at the end.'

I pulled it out and opened it at the first page. There I was. Serious little face. Wispy brown bob. I showed Mum. 'When was this taken?' I asked, trying to sound casual.

'Just after we got you,' she said. 'Christmas time.'

This was the best I was going to get. 'Can I take it?'

'Sure,' Mum said. 'But make sure you bring it back.' She smiled. 'Those pictures are precious.'

I stood up. 'I'll be back in a minute.' I looked from Mum to Jam. He stared back at me suspiciously. 'I just want to scan this in.'

I raced back up to Mum's study and pulled up the *Missing-Children.com* site. I held the photo of me next to the picture on the screen of Martha Lauren Purditt. I think I'd expected this would prove things one way or the other.

It didn't.

Martha Lauren was chubby and dimpled and laughing.

In the photo from Mum's album my face was thinner and I wasn't smiling.

And yet there were similarities: the shape of the eyes, the crease under the lips. It could be me. It all, almost, fitted.

I felt like I was on one of those funfair rides that spin you round in so many directions at once that you can't tell which way is up.

If that *was* me, I wasn't who I thought I was. I had a different name. A different nationality. Even a different birthday. None of the facts of my life were certain.

'What are you doing?' Jam was staring at me from the doorway, a puzzled expression on his face.

'Nothing.' I quickly minimised the screen.

I was being ridiculous. The whole thing was too bizarre. Jam would laugh at me if I told him – tell me to beam back up to planet Egotrip or something. And yet I wanted to show him. I wanted to know what he thought.

'Don't give me that.' Jam narrowed his eyes. 'You've been freaking out since I got here. All that crap with the photo albums. You just wanted me out of this room.'

'No I didn't, Jam.' I tried to smile. 'It was just this weird – thing . . .' I tailed off.

Jam walked over to the computer. 'What kind of weird thing?' He grinned, but the grin didn't quite reach his eyes. 'Like some weird guy asking you out? What did you say?'

'What? No. Ew. No way.' What was Jam going on about? He knew I was, like, totally uninterested in dating and boys and all that stuff.

'Then why . . . ?' Jam's eyes focused on the minimiser lozenge at the bottom of the screen. 'Why are you looking at a missing children site?'

'Promise you won't laugh?'

He nodded. I clicked on the minimiser lozenge. Martha Lauren Purditt appeared on the screen. Jam glanced from her to the photograph of me on the desk beside the computer.

He frowned. 'What?' His eyes widened. 'You don't think that's you, do you?'

I looked away, my cheeks burning. 'I don't know,' I whispered.

I looked up. Jam was clicking on a link marked: *age-progressed photograph.*

'Wait,' I cried out.

But it was too late. A new picture was on the screen, showing Martha Lauren Purditt as she might appear now. I didn't want to look at it and yet I couldn't stop myself.

It was me. But at the same time, it wasn't. The face was too long and the nose too cutesy and turned-up looking.

'Mmmn,' Jam said. 'It's hard to say, isn't it? I mean it looks a bit like you. But . . .'

My heart was beating fast. OK, so he wasn't any more certain than I had been. But at least he wasn't laughing at me.

I wasn't sure whether to be relieved or disappointed.

Without looking at me, Jam clicked back to the first picture and pressed the print icon.

As the printer spewed out the page, Jam held it up to show me. 'It's like a "missing" poster,' he said. 'And look – there's a phone number at the bottom here. Maybe you should call up and—'

'No. No way.' I jumped up and tore the paper out of his hand. This was all moving too fast. Jam was being too practical. Too logical about everything. 'I need time to think,' I said.

'Chill out, Lazerbrain.' Jam rolled his eyes – like he does when his mum and sisters start screaming at each other. 'I was only trying to help. Don't you want to find out if that's really you?'

'Maybe.' I shrugged. The truth was that I didn't know. I didn't know anything any more.

'I guess your mum and dad might be able to tell.' Jam put his head to one side and studied the picture.

'I'm not showing them,' I gasped.

'Yeah. S'probably not a good idea, anyway.'

'What d'you mean?'

'Well.' Jam hesitated. 'If that Martha Lauren girl is you, how d'you think it happened? I mean, back then when you were three, how did you go from being in America in September to being in London by Christmas?'

I shook my head. Trust Jam to start asking all the practical questions. I couldn't even get my head around the idea that I might be a completely different person.

'Think about it, Lazerbrain,' Jam smiled weakly. 'Children don't just vanish for no reason. You must have been taken deliberately.'

'What's that got to do with my mum and dad?' I asked.

Jam took a deep breath. 'I think you have to consider the possibility that your parents were somehow involved.'

3

The secret

I was sure Jam was wrong. Mum and Dad are interfering. And annoying. And old. But there's no way they could have done anything as illegal and wrong as kidnapping a little girl.

Still. When someone plants an idea in your head, it stays there. You can't unthink it.

Was I Martha Lauren Purditt?

I thought about it all the time. I kept the 'missing' poster Jam had printed out under my mattress. I took it out every night and read it over and over until I knew every line of that little girl's face. Every date and detail about her life. Not that there was much to go on.

Several times I picked up the phone to call the number at the bottom of the poster. But I never had the guts to make the call. What was I going to say? *Hi there. I think I might be a missing girl on your website, only with a different birthday and a different first name – oh, and from a different country.*

They'd laugh at me. So would the police.

A week went past. Jam swore he wouldn't tell anyone. It was our secret. But it burned inside me like one of those trick birthday candles you can't blow out.

And then – by accident – I learned something that changed everything for ever . . .

Dad has a bit of a routine when he gets in from work. He doesn't like anyone to speak to him while he changes and pours himself a drink. Then he and Mum have dinner before Dad falls asleep watching TV.

They're always nagging me to eat with them. Mostly it's the last thing I want to do, but it shuts Mum up. And it massively annoys Rory, who has to go to bed before we eat.

That night, Rory appeared in the doorway just as Mum was putting a big casserole dish down on the table.

'Mum, I'm still hungry,' he whined.

Dad rolled his eyes. He gets well narked with Rory's attention-seeking ways. I could see him building up to saying something. (He doesn't exactly operate at the speed of light, my dad.)

But Mum – so strict when it comes to *my* bedtimes – had already taken Rory's side.

'I can't let him go to sleep hungry, Dave.'

And before Dad could say anything, she'd grabbed the fruit bowl and was shushing Rory out the door.

Dad stared at the casserole dish as if he was hoping the stew inside would somehow leap out onto his plate.

'She spoils that boy,' he muttered under his breath.

I grinned to myself. Dad's the supreme master of the blindingly obvious comment. He's an accountant – good with Maths homework but a bit slow when it comes to words.

Which is what made his next sentence so jaw-droppingly, outstandingly incredible.

'Mum tells me you were asking about your . . . about when you were little,' he said.

I nearly choked on the slice of bread and butter I'd been stuffing into my mouth.

'Well?' Dad had his serious face on. Not an easy one for him to pull off as he's short and bald with round, pink cheeks.

I could feel the heat creeping up round my neck. I looked away and nodded.

Dad cleared his throat. 'I think . . .' he said. Long pause.

Come on, Dad. Before we both die of old age. Please.

'I think . . . that if you're old enough to ask—'

At that moment Mum reappeared. She took one look at my red face and I knew she knew what was going on.

'Old enough to ask what?' she said.

Dad mumbled something totally incoherent. Mum put her hands on her hips.

'I thought we agreed, Dave?' she said in a threatening voice.

The atmosphere in the room stretched out tight, like a Croydon facelift.

I pushed back my chair and stood up, my hands balled at my sides. If she was going to stop Dad from talking to me, she could forget about me eating her stupid stew.

'Sit down, Lauren,' Mum snapped.

Anger surged up from my stomach. 'No,' I shouted. 'Who put you in charge? Why d'you always, always think you know what's best for everyone else?'

Mum's face clenched up.

'Sit down and eat. Now.'

Tears of rage and frustration welled in my eyes. How dare she order me about like that – like a little kid. 'I won't sit down,' I shouted. 'You can't tell me what to do. You're not even my real mother.'

I ran out of the kitchen, slamming the door behind me. Tears streamed down my face as I raced through the hall, heading for the stairs and the small privacy of my own room.

Rory was sitting on the top step, munching on an apple.

'Why's everyone shouting?' he said.

I stopped just below him and took a deep breath. My hands shook as I wiped my face. 'Get out of my way,' I muttered.

'Wanna see a Martian train wreck?' Rory opened his mouth and stuck out a tongue full of pale-green mush.

I closed my eyes. What had I done to deserve such an uncool family? I bet Martha Lauren Purditt's family weren't like this. I could just imagine them: understanding, glamorous mother; sensitive, fun-loving father; and not a brother or sister in sight.

The sound of Mum and Dad's angry voices drifted towards the stairs.

Rory shuffled down a couple of steps towards me. 'Are Mum and Dad going to get divorced?' he said.

'Yeah,' I snapped. 'They're arguing over which one of them has to live with you afterwards.'

Rory stuck his tongue out at me again but didn't say anything. A few seconds later he stomped off to his room.

The shouting was getting louder, Mum's high-pitched shriek piercing through Dad's thundering rumble. And then I heard my own name. I walked back across the hall, trying to separate out what they were saying.

'Stop shouting,' Mum was yelling. 'This is your fault. You promised me—'

'For Chrissakes!' Dad yelled back. 'I'm only saying we can't ignore her asking about it.'

I'd never heard him sound so angry. I mean, they bicker all the time, but mostly about trivial stuff – like Dad working too hard. This was different.

I shivered, and crept closer to the kitchen door.

There was silence for a few seconds. Then Mum spoke again. Her voice was quieter now, almost pleading.

'She's too young. Her head's still full of homework and . . . and . . . pop songs.'

Yeah, right, Mum – you know me so well.

'Then why's she so angry? Why's she been asking questions?' Dad said.

'Some stupid school project got her started. But she'll lose interest.'

There was a pause.

'You mean you hope she'll lose interest.'

There was a longer pause. Then I could hear Mum sniffing. Her voice sounded muffled.

'If we tell her one thing, she'll want to hear the rest.'

Dad murmured something I couldn't catch.

'I know, but not now,' Mum said. 'When she's sixteen, I'll show her my diaries. That'll put it all in context for her.'

I heard footsteps coming towards the door and scurried away, up the stairs. My heart was beating fast. So much for all Mum's 'closed adoption' crap. They *did* know something about my life before they got me.

My stomach twisted into a knot. What could it be that was so terrible they didn't think I could handle yet? Could it have anything to do with Martha Lauren Purditt?

I lay on my bed sure of only one thing. There was no way I could wait until I was sixteen to read Mum's diaries.

4

Marchfield

Break time the next day. Jam and I were out on the high street, buying our lunch. It's something school only lets you do once you get to Year Ten. Three weeks in and Mum's already complaining about my eating rubbish food – and spending too much money on it.

I told Jam about the diaries while we waited to order our pizza from the takeaway bar.

'Why don't you just go and read them?' he said.

'Because Mum keeps all her old stuff in these locked trunks up in our attic.'

A gust of wind whipped round my legs as a group of girls from another school tottered into the pizza bar. They stood in a cluster at the opposite end of the counter from us, giggling over a menu.

Jam ordered our usual – a ham and pineapple pizza with double extra pepperoni for me to pick off – then we sat down to wait on the metal bench in the corner.

'Well, get the keys and go up there,' he said.

I stared at him. Jam always made everything sound so simple.

'What about Mum?' I said. 'I'll need someone to keep her out of the way for at least an hour.'

Jam frowned. 'Doesn't she ever go out?'

'Not much.' It was true. While Dad often doesn't get in until nine or so, Mum works from home and spends most weekends and evenings in her office too.

She isn't exactly a party animal.

After a few minutes Jam wandered over to the counter to see where our pizza was. While he waited, one of the girls from the other school went up to him. She was dead hard-looking, with spiky blonde hair and her school skirt hitched right up her legs.

'My mate reckons you're really fit,' she said, jerking her thumb towards a short redhead on the edge of the group of girls.

I grinned as Jam blushed. He was always getting hit on by girls. I guess he is quite good-looking. Tall, with regular features and lovely smooth, golden skin.

The hard-faced blonde put her hand on her hip. 'So d'you wanna go out with her? She's free tomorrow night,' she said. There was a burst of giggles from the group at the other end of the counter.

Jam was smiling, trying to be nice as he said no. He looked really embarrassed. The man approached with our pizza.

I stood up and took the box. Then I turned to the girl. 'Sorry.' I touched Jam's arm. 'But he's busy tomorrow night.'

I let go of Jam and swept out of the shop. There was a chorus of sarky 'Ooooo's at my back. I smiled to myself again.

It was funny how alike Jam and I were. Not interested in going out with anyone, just wanting to be friends. Well, friends with each other.

Jam caught up with me as I set off up the high street.

'What did you mean?' he said. 'About tomorrow night?'

I grinned at him. 'I was hoping you'd help me get Mum out of the way so I can look through those diaries.'

My plan was simple. Jam's mum, Carla, was always saying she and my mum should get together, what with me and Jam being such good friends. So that night, after school, I asked her if Mum could visit her the very next day.

'She'd really like to get to know you,' I lied.

Carla was typically enthusiastic, if a little vague: 'How lovely, darling, but tell her to come before seven, that's when I start seeing clients.'

Of course Mum didn't want to go. Partly because she hates going anywhere. And partly because she thinks Jam's mum is a total nut. She's right, in fact – but that's another story.

'What does "come before seven" mean?' Mum said. 'Suppose they're having tea when I get there?'

I sighed. 'They don't "have tea" like that. They all just drift in and out, getting food when they want it. Come on, Mum. Please. It'll be really embarrassing if you won't go.' In the end Mum agreed.

I reckoned Carla would keep Mum talking for at least an hour. Plenty of time for me to find the diaries in the attic and have a good look at them.

Mum left our house at quarter past five the next day, still grumbling and issuing instructions about Rory not having chocolate before tea. Ten minutes later, Jam rang from his house.

'The package has arrived,' he said.

I giggled. 'Don't forget to ring me as soon as she leaves again,' I said.

As soon as Jam hung up, I raced down to the kitchen to grab as much chocolate as I could carry. I panted back up the stairs and into Rory's room. His pudgy little face was bent over his PSP. Jam – in a heroic gesture of friendship – had lent him his *Legends of the Lost Empire* game.

'Here.' I thrust the chocolate bars at him. 'Now keep quiet.'

I picked up my mobile and charged into Mum's office.

All her keys hung neatly on a row of hooks behind the desk. I shoved the set marked 'attic' in my pocket, then ran into Mum and Dad's room, pulled down the loft ladder and climbed up.

I'm guessing, of course, but I imagine most people's attics are a bit of a mess. Bin bags, bits of old equipment, suitcases. That kind of stuff.

Not ours.

Mum has everything organised in trunks. Labelled trunks. *Clothes. School. University. Letters.* There. *Diaries.*

My hands were shaking as I fumbled with the keys, trying one after the other in the lock. At last one of the keys turned with a satisfying click. I opened the trunk and peered inside at the neatly stacked rows of black notebooks. They were labelled in quarter years: *Jan–Mar*, *Apr–Jun* and so on.

All disgustingly well-organised.

I rummaged around and found the year I was adopted. I picked out *Sep–Dec*: the three months that covered Martha's disappearance and my own adoption.

Heart pounding I scanned the pages, searching for my name.

There were references to me on *Sept 25* and *30.* But at that point I was just a possibility. An idea of a child they hadn't met. Then . . .

Oct 7 – We met Lauren at Marchfield. She smiled at me. At least I'm telling myself it was a smile. Dave said it was more of an accidental curl of the lip. Lauren doesn't smile much. Not surprising, I suppose. With Sonia Holtwood involved, everything's very tense and I'm sure she picks up on it.

I put the diary down. For the first time since I'd found the information about Martha Lauren Purditt on the net, I wasn't sure if I wanted to know any more. My stomach twisted into a knot. Who was Sonia Holtwood? And what exactly were they all involved in?

I sat there for a few moments, the diary in my lap.

Then I picked it up again. It was too late to turn back now.

Oct 14 – I daren't hope. I don't want to be disappointed again . . .

Oct 20 – Sonia's attitude is unbelievable. But we're going to go ahead anyway. Nothing's going to stop us getting Lauren. Nothing.

Oct 30 – Lauren. My Lauren. After all this time, it's really happening. We're bringing her home from Marchfield in two days.

That was it. No more references to Sonia or Marchfield.

Just loads of stuff about what it was like when they got me home.

So what and where was Marchfield? I flicked to the back of the diary, to a clear plastic sleeve containing a selection of business cards. I saw it instantly – a yellowing card with the words Marchfield Adoption Agency embossed across the front.

The doorbell rang – a long continuous screech.

I leaped up and raced to the trapdoor.

'Hi, Jam,' I heard Rory saying.

'Lauren! She's almost here.' Jam's yell echoed urgently up from the hall.

I pocketed the Marchfield Agency business card, tossed the diary back in the trunk and raced down the stepladder. Jam pelted into Mum and Dad's bedroom in time to help me push the stepladder back up into the attic. It clicked into place just as the front door shut.

'I'm home,' Mum shouted.

'Why didn't you call me?' I said to Jam, as I carefully replaced the keys on their hook.

'I did. Your phone kept going to voice mail. I had to run all the way here – the long way round, too.'

I checked my mobile. The volume was turned right down.

Rory was standing in the study doorway, grinning at me. 'I did it while you were getting my chocolate,' he said.

'You little . . .' I lunged for him, but he slipped out of my grasp.

'Do anything and I'll tell Mum you were looking at her things,' he said.

I stared at him. 'Fine.' I'd get him back some other way.

We went downstairs. Jam slipped out, unnoticed by Mum. She was in a good mood, clattering about in the kitchen. I suspected Carla had given her more to drink than a cup of tea.

'Totally chaotic,' Mum said. 'Poor Jam. They live in the most unbelievable mess. Frankly, the place could do with a damn good clean as well. But of course, Carla's too busy with her hypno-flexology-colour-in-your-own-aura nonsense.'

I nodded without really listening. My mind was on the Marchfield business card in my pocket. I slipped out of the kitchen and went up to my room.

Hands shaking, I took out the card:

Taylor Tarson, Director
Marchfield Adoption Agency
11303 Main Street
Marchfield, Vermont, USA.

America. I was adopted from America?

The 'missing' poster from the website flashed into my mind. Martha Lauren was American too. My skin erupted in goosebumps, sending a shiver snaking down my back.

I was getting closer and closer to the truth.

Part of me wanted to run back downstairs, burst into the kitchen and confront Mum with what I'd found out. But what good would it do?

She's too young.

Mum still wouldn't tell me anything.

Plus – she would totally freak if she knew I'd been nosing through her diaries.

Whatever I was going to find out from the Marchfield Adoption Agency, I would have to find out alone.

5

Carla

The last week of September was hot and sunny. With the weather like that, I much preferred being at Jam's house to mine. The grass in his back garden was always long and soft – perfect for lying out on.

The day after I'd read Mum's diaries, we rushed back there after school. I reckoned we should be able to sit outside for at least an hour before Mum rang to demand I went home and did my homework.

As I sat down on the grass, Jam emerged from the kitchen carrying a bunch of bananas, three vegetarian sausages and several packets of biscuits.

'So how far away from each other are Marchfield and Evanport?' he asked, ripping open one of the biscuit packs.

'Not far – just a few centimetres on Rory's atlas.' I tipped my face to the sunshine. 'They're in different states, though.'

Jam carefully placed a veggie sausage between two wholewheat digestives. 'What're you going to do?' he said.

'I don't know,' I sighed.

What options did I have? I couldn't talk to Mum and Dad. And I already knew no adoption agency would tell me anything without their approval.

Marchfield wasn't even in this country, for God's sake.

Everywhere I turned was a dead end.

I detached a banana from the bunch and broke off the tip.

'That all you're having?'

I shrugged. It's not like I'm a diet freak or anything. But I hate being so much bigger than the rest of my family. I mean, Mum's basically a bony elbow on legs. I'm even taller than Dad.

Jam stretched out across the grass and bit into his sausage and biscuit sandwich. 'You know, Laurenzo. It's a shame you can't *remember* all this stuff about your adoption. It would save an awful lot of time.'

I stared at him. For some reason it had never occurred to me that the one place all the answers to my past could be found was inside my own head.

The front door slammed. Jam sat up and groaned. 'The lunatic has re-entered the asylum.'

A minute later Carla poked her frizzy head round the back door. 'I'm back from my colonic, darlings.'

I blushed.

'Gross, Mum.' Jam made a face. 'Way too much information.'

Carla stepped out into the garden and fluffed up her hair. 'Don't be so uptight, darling. I'm sure Lauren's heard it all before. What are *you* guys doing?' Her eyes twinkled.

Jam's face went red. 'Mu-um,' he muttered.

Carla winked at me.

'Just so you know,' she said, 'I have a new client at seven-thirty, for which I will need Absolute Quiet.'

She padded inside again.

Jam flopped back onto the grass. 'Could she *be* more embarrassing? Last week I caught her telling that new games teacher how she'd unblocked some woman's energy through her big toe.'

I giggled. 'Sounds painful,' I said. Then my eyes snapped wide open. 'Maybe your mum could help me remember my early life? I mean all that stuff she does – rebirthing, reflexology, hypnotherapy – it's got to—'

'No way.' Jam stared at me. 'My mum's a nut job.'

'Come on, Jam,' I wheedled. 'It's worth a try. She might help me.'

'Help you go insane, you mean.'

There was no convincing him, so I wandered into the kitchen by myself. Carla was standing at a cupboard, pulling out a baking tray.

'Can I ask you something?' I said.

'Sure.' She indicated I should sit down, then placed a bowl full of an oily, orangey sludge in front of me.

Last time I was here, Carla had made nut cutlets in the shape of parts of the body. We had to guess which they were. 'A little Biology homework, darlings.'

I wondered what the sludge in the bowl was.

'Homemade hummus,' Carla announced, handing me a wooden spoon. 'Go on, stir,' she said.

I picked up the spoon and looked at her, hesitantly.

'So you've been thinking about your birth parents?' Carla said, sitting down beside me.

My jaw dropped. 'Did Jam say something . . . ?'

'Oh for goodness' sake.' Carla shook her head so hard all her frizzy curls trembled. 'He's a man. Strong and silent, God love him. No. It was Mrs Worrybags.'

For a second I had no idea who she meant. Then my eyes widened.

'My *mum* told you?' I said, incredulously.

'Not exactly.' Carla shook her bangles down her arm. 'But I use my intuition for a living. I can see the signs.'

I picked up the wooden spoon and stirred the slimy, orange hummus. 'What signs?'

Carla waved her hand vaguely. 'Oh, darling. The point is, how can I help?'

I could feel my face reddening. I loved the way Carla treated kids like adults – but the truth was, I was just a teensy bit scared of her. She was so different from my mum.

I took a deep breath. Then it all tumbled out in a rush: 'I was wondering if you could hypnotise me and I could find out about my real mother, my real family. About before I was adopted.'

Carla arched her eyebrows. 'And what d'you think Mrs Worrybags would say to that?'

I blushed.

Carla stared at me. She seemed torn, unsure what to do. 'I suppose I could put you in a state of deep relaxation,' she mused. 'It couldn't hurt.'

I stared back at her, now torn myself. What had seemed like the obvious thing to do, in the glare of the afternoon sunshine, now felt a bit silly. Scary, even.

I opened my mouth to say perhaps it wasn't such a good idea, but Carla jumped up impulsively. 'Oh, come on then. If we're going to do it, let's do it now.'

My heart leaped into my throat. 'No,' I squeaked. 'Not right now. Not yet.'

Carla tossed back her hair. 'Better now than when you've had a chance to create internal blockages. Come on.'

She strode out of the kitchen. I had no choice but to follow.

6

The memory

I realised I was in deep trouble when Carla started introducing me to her candles.

'This is Evie, this is Elsie and this is Tom,' she said, pointing to three stout wax balls, ranged in saucers across a low shelf. 'At least this is the home of their spirit-flame. They are drawn to the fire, here in my Room of Utter Peace. Let their spirits enfold you, take you into another space and time.'

Carla's Room of Utter Peace – or Room of Utter Piss, as Jam liked to call it – was at the top of the house, a converted attic. There was one tiny window and the walls sloped down to the floor on both sides, giving the room a cosy, shadowy feel.

The downstairs noises – TV and Jam's sisters arguing – fell away as Carla shut the door. She indicated I should sit on one of the low, purple-cushioned chairs in the corner.

'Don't look so nervous,' she smiled. 'I'm not going to brainwash you.'

'What *are* you going to do?' I said. I was totally

regretting having said anything to her. What was I thinking? I didn't want anyone poking about inside my brain, seeing all my secret thoughts – especially not Jam's weirdo mum.

'I told you. I'm going to put you in a state of deep relaxation where you'll be able to remember things that are buried far down in your psyche.'

'Will I know what you're doing?' I asked.

'Of course. I'm just helping you relax. You're in control the whole time.'

I sat back in one of the chairs. Carla began by getting me to imagine I was lying on my back in an empty field.

'Feel the touch of the grass under your hands; smell the sweet, fresh air . . .'

Sounds weird, I know. But actually it was kind of fun. After a while, I found myself really getting into it.

Carla cleared her throat. Her bangles jangled like wind chimes. 'I'm going to count backwards from ten,' she said in this low, soothing voice. 'With each number you're going to let go, feel your body sink into a deep sleep. But your higher consciousness will stay awake and alert. Ten. Nine. Eight . . .'

With each number my body sank lower and lower into the chair. I felt deliciously soft and relaxed.

'. . . Three. Two. One.'

My whole body sank down, deep against the chair. It

was the strangest feeling. My body was asleep. But I was, like, totally awake.

'Good, good,' Carla's voice was a soft drone. 'Now you are three years old. What do you see?'

At first I didn't see anything. I tried imagining being three. Teddy bears. Ball pits. Playing with dolls. Nothing.

Jeez. This was a total waste of time.

I stopped trying and just let myself be heavy in the chair.

Then, without warning, an image popped into my head. I was little. Very little. I had a red plastic bucket in my hand. The ground was yellow. It moved under my feet.

'Where are you now?' Carla said.

In my memory I wriggled my toes. Sand. I was on a beach. The sun shone. The sea roared behind me. I waved at a woman further up the beach. The sun glinted on her hair, on her white dress. She looked like an angel. But she was real. She waved at me. She laughed. Then she turned away and ran towards some rocks. Her long black hair streamed down her back. I dropped the bucket. I had to follow her. Find her. See her face.

'Lauren, Lauren.' As Carla's voice brought me back to the present, the woman in my memory vanished. A sense of terrible, swamping loss flooded through me.

'I'm going to count up to ten,' Carla said. 'With each number your body will awaken. By the time I reach ten you will be fully awake.

'. . . Eight, Nine, Ten.'

I opened my eyes. I was back in the Room of Utter Peace. Evie, Elsie and Tom were winking at me from their shelf.

There was a crushing weight on my heart.

Carla smiled encouragingly. 'How do you feel?' she asked.

Empty. Sad. Alone.

'Fine,' I said. 'Nothing happened though.'

Carla fluffed out her hair. 'Never mind, darling. We can always try again another time.'

I curled the memory up in my hands. I was Martha. And the dark-haired woman on the beach was my real mother. I had no proof. But in my heart I was sure.

I couldn't stop thinking about her. Before, I'd *wanted* to know about my past. Now I totally *needed* to know.

I lay awake most of that night, trying to decide what to do. It all came down to the Marchfield Agency. I checked on the net – it was still in Vermont. Taylor Tarsen was still director.

I knew my adoption file would be stored there. Surely that would contain clues about what really happened?

Yes. That file was my starting point. And if the agency wouldn't show it to me, I was just going to have to go to Marchfield and steal a look at it for myself.

Whatever it took.

7

Holiday

Rory was in the living room, whirling about with a toy sword. His current obsession is *Legends of the Lost Empire.* Not just the film, which he's dragged Dad to three times, but the book (on audio CD, natch) and the PC game. We even have to have this revolting cereal so he can collect all the *Legends of the Lost Empire* plastic characters.

'Show me your moves, Rory,' I said.

Rory's eyes narrowed. 'Why?'

'Go on,' I smiled. 'I want to see. Who are you being now? Is that the troll?'

Rory shot me a look of utter contempt. 'Trolls don't carry swords. This is Largarond, the elf king of Sarsaring.' He raised the sword above his head. 'This is him in killer mode.'

'Fantastic,' I enthused. 'You look way cool doing all that.'

Rory said nothing. But as he did the move again, a smile curled across his mouth.

I sat and watched for another minute or so. I felt a pang

of guilt for what I was about to do. But then I reminded myself how Rory had deliberately turned down the volume on my phone the other day.

He deserved what he got.

I moved in for the kill.

'There's an awesome *Legends of the Lost Empire* ride just opened at the Fantasma theme park,' I said.

Rory stopped his sword in mid-swing. 'What's it like?' he said.

'Wicked.' I knew the ride existed but I was a bit hazy on the exact details. I thought fast. 'There's this big, dark forest and you go through it really fast, spinning round. And . . . and if you're sitting up at the front you get to fight all the main characters.'

Rory frowned. 'But the main characters should all be fighting the troll army and the goblin hordes of Nanadrig.'

'They do,' I said quickly. 'I meant you're *with* all the main characters, fighting the baddies. Jam told me about it. He says its awesome.'

Though I say it myself, that last bit was massively clever of me. Rory adores Jam. And anything Jam thinks is cool, Rory wants to do too.

'I want to go on the ride,' Rory said, lunging forward with his sword.

'Well, you'll have to ask Mum,' I said, trying to hide a smile. 'The Fantasma theme park's in America.'

It was in New Hampshire to be exact, near the capital, Concord. I'd spent the whole of the previous evening looking for a holiday destination which was as close to Vermont as possible. Fantasma was perfect – a newish theme park specialising in indoor rides connected to fantasy stories. Lots of fairy-tale type stuff, plus a brand new ride celebrating the massive success of the *Legends of the Lost Empire* film, book and revolting-cereal franchise.

Once I'd sorted Rory, Mum was the next step. I reminded her casually how she'd been saying for months that we should take a family holiday.

'I know, but we're planning on buying a new car this year,' Mum said. 'We can't afford that *and* a holiday.'

'But a holiday where we can all be together's more important,' I said. 'Who cares if our car's a bit old?'

Mum raised her eyebrows. 'Well, *you* did the last time I came to pick you up from a party in it. You said it was so old it was embarrassing. Which you also said made it remind you of me.'

'I'm sorry I said that,' I muttered. 'I was being stupid. It's just, well, there won't be that many more family holidays will there? I mean, soon I'll just be too old. Don't you want to make the most of it while I still really want us all to be together?'

She looked up at me. And I knew I had her.

The rest was easy. What with Rory going on and on about the *Legends of the Lost Empire* ride, and me quoting whole passages out of the New Hampshire tourism website about the extraordinary and sublime beauty of the area's autumnal landscape, Mum quickly came to believe that a trip to the north-east coast of America was the ideal half-term break.

'It's still going to be expensive,' she said grimly.

I was ready for this. 'Doesn't need to be,' I said. 'I've checked. They're doing special offers at the theme park. And Jam and I were looking into cheap flights on the internet last night.'

Mum nodded, thoughtfully.

'You know, Dave, we could all do with a holiday,' she said to my dad that evening. 'It's been two years since we went anywhere as a family.'

Dad mumbled a bit about his holiday allowance at work. But I could see that if Mum wanted to go, he wasn't going to put up much of a fight.

I showed them the travel research Jam and I had done. 'We'll have to wait a couple of hours to change planes in Boston,' I said. 'But the flights are really cheap.'

It had taken us ages to work out all the connecting flights. Boston was the closest big place to Vermont that I could see on the map. While Mum and the others were waiting for their flights up to New Hampshire, I could get a flight from Boston to Burlington in Vermont, and then a bus to Marchfield.

All I needed was money.

For the next few days I worked my butt off, running errands for our neighbours and doing all the food shopping for Mum. We were due to fly out early on the Friday morning that half-term started – missing one whole day of school. Jam came round to see me on the Tuesday evening before. I was in my bedroom, sorting out the backpack I was going to take with me to Marchfield.

I knew something was up as soon as Jam appeared in the doorway. His face was red and he was, very self-consciously, holding something behind his back.

'What's going on?' I said.

Jam held out his hand. There, in the palm, were two crisp hundred-dollar bills.

'Where d'you get that?'

Jam shrugged. 'Paper round, birthday – plus my nan sent me a bit. And I was saving up for a computer.'

I bit my lip. I knew how much Jam wanted a computer of his own. He hated having to share the family PC with all his sisters.

'You are such a friend, Jam,' I said. 'I'll pay you back, I promise.'

He smiled. 'Maybe, when you get back—'

Then Mum started shouting downstairs.

I ran out of my bedroom.

'You can't do this, Dave,' Mum yelled.

I'd worked out what was wrong before my feet hit the bottom step: Dad was saying he was too busy at work to go on the holiday.

Sure enough, as I raced into the kitchen I caught the words: 'But it's the biggest client the firm's ever had.'

Mum and Dad both looked at me.

Mum wiped her hands furiously on a tea towel. 'You tell her,' she spat.

Dad hung his head. He mumbled something about work pressure and a big new contract, but I wasn't listening. I had worked so hard to be ready for this trip. And now here was Dad telling us he couldn't go.

Mum was watching me, twisting the tea towel round her hand.

When Dad finished speaking I turned to her. 'But you, me and Rory can still go, can't we?' I said.

Mum's jaw tightened. 'If Dad can't come, then it won't be a proper family holiday.' She glared at him. 'So no, we can't go.'

'But . . . but we'll lose all the money if we cancel now.' I couldn't believe it. Simply could not believe that all my plans were falling apart.

Mum pursed her lips.

'This is so totally unfair.' I stormed out of the room. The shouting started again before I got back up to my bedroom. I slammed the door shut and sank onto my bed. Jam was still there, looking out of the window.

The rucksack I had already packed stood in the corner. I could see the edge of my pink purse sticking out the front pocket. I thought of all the money I'd saved up and about Jam, giving me his savings too. Tears welled up in my eyes.

Jam turned round. I didn't need to ask if he had heard what had happened. They'd probably heard three streets away.

'Maybe you could persuade your mum to let someone else take your dad's place,' he said, 'so the money wouldn't be wasted.'

I stared at him. It seemed like a long shot, but it was worth a try. 'Who though?' I frowned. Who would Mum be prepared to take instead of Dad? A brother or sister, perhaps? Except she didn't have one. Maybe a friend?

Jam grinned at me, as if he was waiting for me to get a joke. And then it dawned on me. I rushed back downstairs. Dad was disappearing out the front door. 'Wait,' I shouted. But he didn't stop. Mum was standing at the sink, scrubbing hard at an already sparkling pan. She didn't turn round when I came in.

‘Why can’t Jam come instead of Dad?’ I said.

Mum rubbed her eyes. ‘I don’t think so, Lauren. It’s supposed to be a family holiday. We should reschedule it.’

‘We can’t. Like I said before, if we pull out at this point we won’t get any of the money back.’ I paused. ‘Oh, Mum, of course it would’ve been better with Dad, but you know how responsible Jam is. He can help out in all sorts of ways.’

Mum put down her washing-up brush and turned round to face me. She sighed. ‘I know how much you were looking forward to the holiday. And you’re right, Jam is grown-up for his age, though that’s because Carla puts way too much on his shoulders.’ She paused. ‘But it’s probably too late to change the tickets. Anyway, Jam may not want to come.’

‘It isn’t and he does.’ Every muscle in my body was tensed, ready to swat her arguments away like flies.

Mum sighed. ‘OK, OK, but . . .’ Her face hardened. ‘What about the sleeping arrangements?’ she said, her cheekbones pinking. ‘I mean you’re fourteen. Jam’s just had his fifteenth birthday. I don’t want . . . I mean I won’t have you . . .’

I looked at the floor, heat flushing my throat and face. ‘Mum,’ I said hoarsely. ‘It’s not like that. Jam and I are just friends.’

Mum put her hands on her hips. ‘Is that what Jam thinks?’

'Of course. Anyway, I'll come in with you. Jam can sleep with Rory. Rory'll love it.'

'OK,' she said at last. 'I'll call Jam's mum.'

8

America

My stomach was already in my throat before the steward announced we were beginning our descent into Logan Airport.

The last few days had been beyond hectic. Our tickets were non-refundable, so we had to pay an admin fee to get Dad's ticket switched to Jam's name. This took seven long, frustrating phone calls with Mum muttering pessimistically the whole time that it wouldn't work out. Then there was a nasty panic on Thursday evening when Jam couldn't find his passport. But once we were on the plane, there was nothing to do except think.

And my thoughts led to one, inescapable conclusion: I was utterly, totally mad.

I was planning to find my way round a strange airport, buy a ticket to another strange airport, then take a bus to a place I had never been, to find out information I was sure no one wanted to give me.

I looked across the aisle, to where Jam was explaining some *Legends of the Lost Empire* PSP move to an enraptured Rory. He must have sensed me watching him, because he looked up and smiled.

No way would I have admitted it to another living soul, but the truth was I'm not sure I'd have had the guts to go through with my plan if I hadn't had Jam with me.

Don't get me wrong. I'm no wussy little airhead needing some big strong guy to look after her. I'm used to travelling around London on my own. And I've been on aeroplanes before.

It's just this was a big deal. And I needed a friend to share it with. My best friend.

It took ages to get through customs and immigration. After queueing for nearly an hour we reached the counter and an unsmiling official. He asked us to place our forefingers into a groove on this little box, so there'd be a record of our fingerprints at the airport, then made us stand in front of a tiny camera to have our pictures taken. Every time he looked at me I felt guilty.

Mum was in a right state. She worried about our luggage getting lost. She worried about one of the officials stopping us and dragging us off to be interrogated. And she worried about what she had forgotten and left at home.

By the time we were out in the airport lounge, free to hang out until the connecting flight an hour later, I don't know which of us was more strung out. At least that made it easier for me to persuade Mum to give us some money.

'Jam and I want to have a look round,' I said. 'We're not going to buy anything, but imagine if something happened to you and we couldn't find you later. You'd want us to have some cash on us, wouldn't you?'

Mum pulled a wodge of dollar bills out of her purse and handed them over. 'Emergency use only,' she said sternly.

I nodded, trying to ignore the pinpricks of guilt that stabbed at my conscience.

To me, this is an emergency.

'And for goodness' sake put it in your shoe.' (This is her anti-mugger hiding-place of choice.)

'Can I come with you?' Rory whined.

'No,' I snapped. All of a sudden my nerves felt like they were strained to breaking point.

'But later we'll go and look at the games in the Duty Free shop,' Jam added pacifyingly.

'Much later,' I muttered.

So, with a worried sigh, Mum pecked me on the cheek and reminded me for the tenth time where we were to meet up for the New Hampshire flight.

As I walked away from her I realised my hands were shaking.

'Let's count the money,' Jam said.

I grinned. You could always depend on Jam to get practical when needed. I checked my purse. $523, including the $200 Jam had given me. Plus Jam had $180 from his mum, making $703 in total.

My heart thumped. This was it. Make or break.

'Seems a shame to spend it all on flights and buses,' Jam murmured.

'What?' I said.

He reddened. 'I'm just saying. Hey. Chill. I'm totally cool with this.'

'OK.' I took a deep breath. 'So where do we get tickets for Burlington?'

I couldn't have done it without Jam. Firstly, he was fifteen, and therefore allowed to travel independently. At fourteen, most airlines insisted that I had to be accompanied by someone his age or older. Secondly, Logan Airport was big. Not any bigger than the airports at home. But still really confusing. I'd researched everything on the internet – we needed a ticket each from Boston to Burlington, then another from Burlington back as far as Concord. But finding where to buy them and making sure we had all the right information with us was much harder than I'd expected.

Then there was the ticket-buying itself. We'd got this story planned – how we were cousins, meeting up with family in Vermont. How my dad had given us cash to get our tickets. The busy girl on the desk swallowed it whole, just glancing at our passports and not really listening to us, but my legs were like jelly by the time we got the tickets in our hands.

If Jam hadn't been there, I honestly think I would have given up on the whole idea. But we made it. We bought our tickets. We found the gate. We got on the domestic flight.

As it was taxiing down the runway I checked the time. This part of America was five hours behind the UK – it was only 11am here.

We were due to meet up with Mum soon. I felt another stab of guilt. But if Mum had talked to me, I told myself, we wouldn't need to be doing this.

I turned off my mobile and told Jam to do the same with his. As soon as we'd landed in Burlington I'd text Mum and let her know we were OK. Tell her to go on ahead to New Hampshire. We'd meet her there.

In my heart I knew there was no way on earth Mum would get on a plane without me. But what could I do about that?

It's her own fault. She shouldn't have lied.

Burlington was freezing. We'd seen the snowy mountain tops from the plane, but even so I wasn't prepared for the icy blast that hit us as we walked off the aeroplane. It was the first sign that I hadn't planned everything as well as I thought.

'I wish I'd brought a hat,' I said, tugging my jacket around me. The outside of the airport was all grey concrete, with a huge car park off to one side.

'Look.' Jam pointed to a row of buses. I knew from my internet research which line stopped at Marchfield. Unfortunately, we had to wait nearly two hours for the next bus.

At last, we pulled out of the airport onto wide, empty roads marked with green signs. Beyond the roads were long stretches of frost-tipped fields with huge, snow-covered hills in the distance.

The other cars we passed seemed bigger – longer – than cars at home. But it was the space that got me the most. The roads were so wide, and the land around them went on for ever. Even the sky seemed bigger.

I huddled next to Jam in the back of the bus. I felt strangely calm. We'd done all the difficult stuff getting here. And whatever was going to happen at the adoption agency was ahead of us.

The bus was well heated and, after a while, I felt my head drooping. I slipped into a deep, velvety sleep.

I was on the beach again, stumbling across the sand. I could see the woman with the long, dark hair far ahead of me. She was darting in and out of the rocks, laughing. The sun was shining on my face. I was happy. I scampered across the sand towards the rocks. She was there. I was going to find her now.

I woke up, disoriented. Jam was still asleep, his elbow digging into my side, his head lolling against my shoulder.

I looked out of the window. The open stretches of land had given way to a thick forest of pine trees. I checked the time. Just gone 3 pm. We'd already been travelling for nearly an hour.

Mum. I gulped. I'd completely forgotten about texting her. I fished out my mobile and switched it on. *Oh no.* I scrolled through something like twenty increasingly hysterical text and voice mail messages.

Guilt rose in me again. No. I wouldn't allow myself to feel sorry for her. I quickly tapped in a text: *we r ok, c u l8r*.

I hesitated. I knew the message wouldn't satisfy Mum for a second. But at least she'd know we were all right. I pressed send, then switched the phone off again.

About half-an-hour later we arrived at Marchfield. As we drove through the outskirts of town, past endless rows of low, detached houses, my stomach twisted into a million knots.

Everything depended on the next couple of hours.

The bus driver grinned when we asked if he knew which end of Main Street number 11303 was.

'It's the Marchfield Adoption Agency,' I said.

'Kinda young to be thinking about adopting kids, aren't you?' he chuckled.

I blushed.

Main Street seemed a bit run-down after all the big houses we'd seen earlier – lots of the shops were boarded up and litter was scattered all over the pavement.

The driver dropped us at the top of the road.

'You OK?' Jam said as we watched the bus zoom off.

'Course,' I lied. In fact my legs were shaking so much I wasn't sure if I could even walk. What was I doing? How on earth was I going to find the courage to march into the adoption agency and follow through the plan Jam and I had made?

Jam put his arm round me. I sank against him. My head nestled against his chest. Jam's heart was beating fast under his jumper. I hugged him. He must be feeling pretty scared too.

Somehow, knowing that helped. I pulled away, gritting my teeth. 'OK,' I said. 'Let's go.'

9

Access denied

The agency was at the far end of Main Street. The road got slightly smarter as we walked. Fewer boarded-up buildings and more actual businesses, albeit with grubby windows and peeling paintwork. There seemed to be hardly any people about, though cars roared past constantly.

Back home I'd imagined the agency being a big house set in an elegant lawn. In fact it was just a shabby, concrete office block, with nothing to make it stand out from the other buildings in the road.

I stood outside, my stomach churning like a washing machine.

'Okay, Laurenzo?' Jam squeezed my arm.

I nodded slowly and pushed open the door.

A large woman in an elastic-waist skirt was standing beside the reception desk. 'Hi there. How can I help you guys?'

I gulped. *This is it. Don't screw up.* 'I'm Lauren Matthews. I was adopted from here,' I said, trying to control the shake in my voice. 'I'd like to speak to Mr Tarsen. He did it. I mean, he organised my adoption.'

A flicker of surprise crossed the woman's face. 'OK,' she said slowly. 'Do you have an appointment?'

'No.' I swallowed. 'I just happen to be here . . . on . . . on holiday, so I thought it would be . . . I wondered if I could talk to him.'

The woman frowned. 'We close in ten, honey. Early for the weekend. Why don't you make an appointment for Monday?'

'No.' Jam and I spoke at the same time. Panic rose in my throat. The plan was to get in and out and back to Burlington Airport as quickly as possible. After buying our air and bus tickets we had precisely $43 left. No way could we hold out until Monday.

'Please let me speak to him. *Please*,' I begged. I could feel tears threatening. I blinked them angrily back.

'Well, I'll try him,' the woman said doubtfully. She pointed us to a couch by the desk, then spoke softly into her headset.

We waited. Five minutes passed. Then a buzzer sounded. The woman wheezed as she leaned across the desk. 'Reception?' she said.

She talked quietly again, for a few seconds, then looked up at us, surprised. 'Mr Tarsen's coming down now,' she said.

I'd expected somebody important-looking. But Mr Tarsen was a bit like a mouse – small and slight with a pointy nose. When he shook hands with me, his palms were damp.

'Elevator's over here,' he smiled. His eyes flickered over Jam then back to me. I caught a whiff of musty cologne as he turned away.

My heart thudded loudly in the muffled silence of the lift. The three of us got out on the first floor. Mr Tarsen led us down a long corridor. My eyes were fixed on the back of his neck, where tufts of wiry grey hair poked out of the top of his white polo-neck.

He stopped outside a door marked *Resource Center*.

'I'd like to speak to you alone,' I said. This wasn't strictly true of course. I would much rather Jam stayed with me. But stage one of our plan was for me to keep Mr Tarsen talking, while Jam had a good look round and worked out where my file was.

Mr Tarsen looked mildly surprised. 'OK. Your boyfriend can wait with my assistant,' he said.

'He's not—' I started. But Mr Tarsen was already herding Jam towards the next room along. 'We won't be long,' he said.

He came back and took me into the Resource Center. A long row of filing cabinets led down to a small window. There were a few tatty sofas and a plastic box full of kids' toys in one corner. I perched on the edge of one of the sofas. My mouth was dry. *What the hell am I doing?* I felt like I might puke any second.

Mr Tarsen sat down opposite me. There was a framed poster on the wall behind his head. It was covered with snapshot-style pictures of smiling families with a line written in swirly type at the bottom: *Marchfield makes miracles. Every day.*

I could hear Jam's voice in my head. *Could that* be *any cheesier?* I wished he was with me.

'How can I help you, Lauren?' Mr Tarsen's manner was kindly but businesslike. Like he knew I was upset and was trying to tell me he sympathised, but he didn't have time to deal with me crying.

I told him my story. That I'd been adopted through Marchfield eleven years ago, but that my parents wouldn't tell me anything about my life before that.

I didn't mention Martha Lauren Purditt.

'I really, really need to know where I come from,' I said. 'I thought maybe you could tell me something about my real mother.'

There was a long pause.

Mr Tarsen's smile seemed a little strained. 'I'm sorry, Lauren. I'm afraid I can't help you.'

'Why not?' My gut twisted into a knot. I knew what was coming, but I had to look shocked. Upset. Like I wasn't expecting it.

'Until you're eighteen, you're not entitled to see your original birth certificate without the approval of your parent or guardian. And you've already made it clear your adoptive parents do not approve. I bet they don't even know you're here, do they?'

I blushed. Mr Tarsen shook his head in this really patronising way. 'I'm afraid I would be breaking Vermont State law if I told you anything.'

'Oh,' I said. 'Oh no.' My voice sounded phoney to my ears. I wondered how far Jam had got in his search.

Mr Tarsen stared at me. 'It isn't just your age,' he said. 'I checked your file before I came down. In your particular case, the mother filed a request for non-disclosure immediately after you were adopted. That means she doesn't want you to know who she is or where she is. Ever.'

The knot in my stomach tightened. Was that true? I'd turned up at Marchfield, expecting that I would have to be cagey about what I wanted. After all, it was likely the agency knew at least some part of what had really happened. A seed of doubt now crept into my head. Maybe I'd got the whole thing wrong. Maybe Mum and Dad and the agency were on the level. And I was simply a child whose mother didn't want her.

No. That couldn't be true. I had remembered my mother. I had dreamed of her. She loved me. She hadn't wanted to lose me.

Mr Tarsen fidgeted in his chair. 'I know it's hard,' he said.

'You mean I mightn't ever find out?' I said. 'About my past?'

'I'm sorry not to have been of more help.' Mr Tarsen stood up. His patronising smile deepened. 'But you wouldn't want me arrested now, would you?'

I stared at his white polo-neck.

Maybe for crimes against fashion.

He nodded towards the door.

Do something.

'Can't you tell me anything about my mother?' I said. I knew I was on dangerous ground. The last thing I wanted was to make Tarsen aware of what I knew about Martha, but I had to give Jam more time to snoop about. 'You must have met her?'

Mr Tarsen shook his head. He stood up. Walked to the door. My heart raced. There was no way Jam would have found where my file was by now.

'Wait,' I said. 'What about Sonia Holtwood?' I'd remembered the name from Mum's diaries. I knew it was risky to mention her – after all, whoever she was, she was obviously involved in my adoption in some way. But I was desperate. I had to give Jam more time.

Mr Tarsen stopped with his hand on the door handle. He turned round to face me.

'Where on earth did you get that name from?' he said slowly.

'I saw it written down somewhere,' I said, unable to think of a plausible cover for Mum's diaries. 'Who is she? Someone who worked here? Or my . . . my real mother? Or . . . ?' I looked down, pressing my hands against my jeans to stop them shaking.

There was a long pause. I could feel Mr Tarsen's eyes boring into me. 'What else did you see, Lauren?' he said.

'Nothing.' My face was burning.

Crap. Crap, crap, crap.

There was a long pause.

'Sometimes it's hard for adopted children to accept the truth,' Mr Tarsen said softly. 'So they make up fairy-tales. Foundling stories. Stories about being stolen away from their homes.'

I looked up at him.

'Is that it, Lauren? Is that what you think happened to you?'

I sat silently, my heart pounding. Mr Tarsen stared intently at my face. Did he know what had happened? Or was he simply guessing at what I might be thinking?

He leaned forward. 'Believe me, Lauren. Sonia was simply young and irresponsible and unable to cope with you.'

'So she *was* my mother?' The words came out in a whisper.

Mr Tarsen looked at me with this strange mix of frustration and something else I couldn't read. What was it? Pity? Fear?

'I can see you're not yet prepared to let this go.' He checked his watch. 'But we can't talk about it any more now. Who else knows the two of you are here?'

'No one,' I said. 'Just the bus driver from Burlington.'

Mr Tarsen tugged at the neck of his jumper.

'OK, this is what we'll do.' He fished a leather wallet from his pocket and drew out two notes. 'Take this. Turn left out of the agency. Couple of blocks down Main Street and you'll see the Piedmarch Motel.'

He shoved the money into my hand.

Jeez. $150.

I stared at him. 'You want us to stay here, at a motel?'

Mr Tarsen nodded impatiently. 'You get a good night's rest. Then we'll call up your parents in the morning and get them to come and take you home. They can pay me back later.'

I frowned. What was going on? One minute the man was Captain Law Enforcement. The next he was offering me money and acting like some private parental liaison service. It didn't make sense.

I stood up. Mr Tarsen ushered me through the door.

Jam was waiting outside, by the lift. Mr Tarsen's hand rested on my shoulder, steering me into the lift, then out of the front door.

'Don't worry, Lauren. I'll see you tomorrow,' he said.

And suddenly Jam and I were out on the street, alone. It was dark now. Nearly 5.30 pm. And even colder than it had been before.

I pulled my jacket round me. 'Well?' I said. 'Did you find anything out?'

'Yup.' Jam chewed furiously on his lip. 'I know where your adoption file is. Or at least I know where the index is. But there's no way we'll be able to get a look at it while everyone's still there. We'll have to go back tonight.'

10

Breaking and entering

I sat on the bed in the motel room and dialled room service. I'd never done anything like that before, and I had butterflies in my tummy as I gave the order. Which I guess sounds stupid, considering everything else I'd done – and was planning to do – that day. 'One Piedmarch Burger with extra cheese and bacon. One Piedmarch Burger Lite. Two Diet Cokes. And one portion of chips – I mean fries, please.'

Jam emerged, showered and changed, from the bathroom as I put down the phone.

'Did you get some food?' he said. 'I'm starving.'

I nodded.

We were in the Piedmarch Motel. We hadn't really wanted to come here, but it got too cold to be outside – and we didn't know anywhere else we could go. There were no other places to stay on Main Street. We'd paid up front for the room, raising no more than an eyebrow from the droopy-faced man at the front desk. It was clean but ugly, dominated by the big double bed I was sitting on.

Maybe we shouldn't have chosen the cheapest – and smallest – room available. I suddenly felt embarrassed at the thought of sharing the bed with Jam.

I stared across the room at the tiny wardrobe, which I already knew was empty apart from three wire coat-hangers.

'I don't want to spend the night here,' I said.

Jam shrugged. 'We don't have much choice.'

I made a face, knowing he was right. Our plan was to break into the agency, find my file, then get the bus straight back to Burlington Airport. But the buses didn't run overnight. The first one left at 6.30 am. Which meant we had to time our return to the agency for a couple of hours before that. The middle of the night.

My mind wandered to Mr Tarsen. How much did he really know? And why had he been so helpful all of a sudden? I couldn't work out why he hadn't just made us call Mum there and then – or the police even. Whatever he was up to, the last thing I wanted was to hang around tomorrow morning, waiting for him.

There was a sharp rap on the door.

Jam opened it. A girl with blonde plaits stood in the doorway. She giggled as she handed Jam our room service food tray.

He paid in cash, then put the tray on the table under the window. The girl didn't take her eyes off him as she closed the door.

'That girl was totally checking you out,' I said, glad to change the subject for a minute.

The back of Jam's neck reddened. 'No she wasn't.' He looked round at me. 'Would you mind if she was?'

'Yeah, right,' I pretended to swoon, the back of my hand against my forehead. 'Because I've been fancying you secretly for months.'

Jam's whole face now went bright red.

Crap. Crap. Crap. He thinks I mean it.

'Only joking,' I said hastily.

'Right.' Jam shrugged. He pointed to the Piedmont Burger Lite. 'What the hell is that? Some kind of diet food?'

I glanced at the thin burger wrapped in its skanky sliver of lettuce. It looked a lot less appetising than his extra-cheese-and-bacon burger.

'I'm sure it'll taste OK,' I said unconvincingly.

'Why do girls worry so much about being fat?' Jam snapped. 'If you eat rubbish food you're gonna end up looking rubbish too.'

Whoa. I stared at him. Jam had never, ever, made any comment about how I looked before. My chest tightened.

'Whatever,' I said, not wanting him to see how hurt I was. 'Tell me what Tarsen's secretary said.'

‘I did.’ Jam glared at me for a second. ‘I asked her how they kept all their records. You know, geeky stuff like when they started storing things online. She told me there are still paper files for older contracts and some documents. The index is in the Resource Center.’

There was an awkward silence while Jam ate his burger. I tried to think of something else to say.

D’you really think I look rubbish?

‘So how d’you know where the Resource Center is?’ I said.

Jam wiped his mouth on his sleeve. To my intense relief he grinned at me. And when he spoke the bitterness had gone from his voice. ‘Sometimes, Lazerbrain, I wonder how you manage to cross the road without getting knocked over. The Resource Center was the room you were in today with Mr Tarsen.’

After we’d eaten we both dozed off in our clothes. It was only about 8 pm in Marchfield, but I guess we were both still running on London time – where it was past midnight.

I had the dream again. This time I reached the rocks on the beach. I peered round one, then another. I ached to see her face. But she wasn’t there. My excitement turned to fear. Where was she? Then, at the edge of the furthest rock, I caught a flash of long black hair.

I woke with a start. Jam was still sleeping beside me.

A slick of hair had fallen over his face. It quivered as he breathed out.

I checked the time: 4.10 am. We'd have to go in a minute. I wandered round the room, unsettled by my dream and the thought of what lay ahead. Jam's PSP was lying on the table under the window, next to the food tray. I picked it up. Six short grooves had been scratched into the back panel.

That was weird. I tilted the whole thing towards me, so that the grooves glinted in the light from outside the motel window.

Why would Jam carve notches into his PSP?

'What time is it?' Jam sat up, yawning.

I put the toy back onto the table.

'Time to go,' I said.

Main Street was deserted. Everything was shut and dark – except for a lone twenty-four-hour cab firm halfway down the road.

The pavements were thick with frost, the air bitterly cold. I hugged my fingers under my armpits to warm them as we walked towards the agency.

Jam led me round to the fire escape at the side of the building. He picked up a large stone from the ground, then started climbing to the first floor. I followed, trying to make as little noise as I could on the iron steps.

Jam stopped at the first-floor landing. Above the low railings in front of us was a large window. He held up the stone.

'Ready?'

I nodded. My breath came out ragged and quick, misting in the cold air.

Jam smashed the stone against the window. The noise of the glass shattering crashed into the night. He did it again. Then again. Smaller smashes, as he created a hole big enough for us to crawl through.

My job was to keep a look out. I leaned over the fire escape, peering as far as I could up and down the street at the front of the building. My heart pounded harder with each smash, convinced the noise would wake the whole town. At last it was over. All I could hear was Jam breathing heavily beside me. I listened for the sound of shouts or police sirens.

Nothing. Not even a burglar alarm. That was weird, wasn't it? Surely a place storing important records would have a—

'Come on.'

I turned round. Jam was carefully picking his way through the window.

I followed him through, making sure I didn't cut my hands on the few shards of glass left in the lower pane.

There was no sound from inside the agency.

My mouth was dry as I felt for the carpet of the first-floor corridor.

We were inside.

I rubbed my sweaty hands down the sides of my jeans. The corridor stretched away from us into shadow. Jam was a metre or so in front of me, shrouded in darkness. I followed him past the lift we had used earlier, to the office where I'd talked with Mr Tarsen.

A row of big files stood on a shelf behind the door. We quickly found the records for the year I was adopted.

'Lauren Matthews Ref: B-13-3207,' I read out. 'The "B" is the code for the filing cabinet.'

Jam walked up and down the row of three-drawer cabinets along the far wall. 'Here,' he said, pointing to the second from the window.

He tugged at the top drawer. Then the middle one. 'It's locked.' He turned and stared at me. 'All the drawers are locked.'

I looked quickly round the room. My eyes fell on the 'Marchfield makes miracles' poster on the wall. It had a thin, metal frame.

'We can use this.' I lifted the poster off its hook. With trembling hands I unclipped the back board and carefully removed the glass. I held the frame steady while Jam ripped the side of it away from the top.

'Lucky it wasn't welded,' he whispered. He took the thin

sliver of metal over to the filing cabinet and began working it through the top drawer.

I tiptoed to the door, listening out for any noise. The agency was silent. Creepy. A trickle of sweat ran down my back.

I turned round and stared at the broken bits of frame on the carpet. 'We've ruined this,' I said. 'And their window.'

Jam snorted softly from the filing cabinet. 'So what d'you wanna do? Leave some of Mr Tarsen's money to pay for it?' He breathed out heavily, forcing his weight against the metal frame. 'Come and help me with this.'

It took several minutes to prise open the drawer. We both leaned so hard on the metal lever, driving it back on itself, that I was afraid it would break before it forced the lock. But at last there was a splintering snap. The drawer opened.

I wondered how long we'd been in the agency. Too long already. Heart racing, I pulled the drawer open and began rooting through the files. After a few seconds my throat tightened. 'It's not here,' I said. 'This is A to G.'

Jam stared at me from the door, where he was now listening out for anyone coming. 'Must be in the next one down.'

My heart was totally in my mouth by the time we prised open the second drawer.

I scanned the files inside so quickly I missed my own name twice. Then I saw it. *Lauren Matthews*.

Below the name-marker was a slim green folder, fastened on three sides like an envelope. I reached into the folder. My fingers closed on air.

'It's not here.' I felt deeper inside the folder, desperate for something, anything to be inside it.

'Lauren,' Jam whispered from the doorway.

'Wait.' My hand grasped at a scrap of paper, tucked right in the corner of the folder. I pulled it out.

'Lauren,' Jam whispered again, more urgently. 'Someone's coming. We have to go. Now.'

11

Leaving . . .

I shoved the piece of paper into my pocket. Raced to the door.

The heavy tread of footsteps echoed in the distance.

'Run,' I hissed.

We pelted along the corridor towards the broken window. The footsteps behind us grew louder and faster. I hauled myself out through the jagged frame, tearing my jeans on the glass as I did so.

I could hear Jam panting behind me as we clattered down the fire escape.

I looked back up to the window as I jumped the last few steps. A dark figure was standing, framed by the broken glass, watching us.

It was Mr Tarsen.

My skin erupted in goosebumps. The way he was just standing there. Why wasn't he yelling out? Or chasing us?

We tore back onto Main Street and along to the motel.

'D'you think Tarsen's called the police?' Jam gasped as we let ourselves into the room.

'Dunno.' I shivered, thinking about the way he'd stared at us.

'We gotta get out of here.' Jam picked up his backpack, then took his PSP off the table and shoved it in his pocket.

I checked the time on the clock by the bed. 'It's too early,' I said. 'The first bus doesn't go for another hour.'

'We can't wait,' Jam said. 'We'll have to get a taxi. From that twenty-four-hour place we passed.'

I nodded, mentally going over the money we had left. Just over one hundred dollars. I hoped that would be enough.

We rushed back up the road to the cab company. Main Street was still eerily silent. My mind kept going over what had happened. None of it made sense

Why was my adoption file empty? I could think of only one explanation: Mr Tarsen had guessed we would come looking for it and had taken the contents himself. So why wasn't he here, now? Why wasn't he chasing us?

As we hurried into the taxi office, I remembered the scrap of paper from the bottom of the file. While Jam went to order a cab, I sat down in the waiting area and pulled it out of my jeans pocket.

It was obviously the corner of some official form. Several of the handwritten letters on the right were missing where the paper had been torn.

Apt. 34
10904 Lincoln Hei
Leaving

Jam finished talking to the taxi man and wandered over. 'The guy says they'll have a cab in a couple of minutes. $80 cash.'

I showed him the paper. 'It's an address,' I said. 'Maybe Sonia Holtwood's. Look. I think "Hei" means "Heights". Lincoln Heights.'

Jam frowned. 'But that could be anywhere. And it says "Leaving" underneath. So even if Sonia used to live there, she's obviously not there now.'

I nodded, my mind still on the address. Surely there was no harm in asking if the cab operator knew where Lincoln Heights was.

He was lounging on a stool, his legs propped up on the counter in front of him. As I walked over, he looked up and pushed back his long, greasy fringe. 'Hey,' he drawled. 'I just told your boyfriend. Two minutes.'

'I know,' I said. 'I was just wondering if you knew where this was?' I laid the scrap of paper on the counter.

The man scratched his head. 'I got no idea about Lincoln Heights, but Leavington's ten miles or so,' he said.

I stared at him, then back at the scrap of paper. 'Leaving' wasn't 'leaving'. It was the start of . . .

'Leavington?'

'Yep. It's on the way to Burlington. But I thought you wanted to go straight to the airport?'

My heart pounded. I ran back to Jam.

He was looking out of the window. 'I can't hear any police up by the motel. But if Tarsen's been watching us . . .' He turned and saw my face, all eager. 'What?'

I explained about the address. 'It's got to be Sonia's. She might still be there,' I said, breathlessly.

I'd expected Jam to suggest we went to Leavington immediately. But instead he shook his head.

'Get real, Lazerbrain,' he said. He wasn't smiling.

My heart sank. 'What?'

'This could be anyone's address . . .'

'But it was in my file,' I said.

'Plus it's at least eleven years old.' Jam rolled his eyes. 'Look, we tried to find your file. It wasn't there. What else can we do? Don't you . . . I mean, doesn't it seem to you like you're getting kind of obsessed?'

I don't think I would have felt more shocked if he'd slapped me. 'No.' I blinked and stepped away from him. 'I'm not obsessed.'

'Then why do you want to go to an old address on a random scrap of paper? It's ridiculous.'

'No it's not,' I said, stung. 'If it was in my file, then it must have something to do with my adoption. And Mr

Tarsen virtually admitted Sonia Holtwood was my mother, so . . .'

'Even if the address *is* to do with your adoption, if you were stolen from your real family it's not likely to be genuine, is it?'

I was sure he was wrong. But what he said sounded so logical I couldn't see how to disagree with it.

'Fine,' I snapped. 'Thanks for your help.'

Jam turned on me. 'Jesus, Lauren,' he hissed. 'I've just broken into a building for you. How much more help d'you want?'

I stared at him, my breathing fast and my jaw clenched. 'If that's how you feel about it, I'll go there by myself.'

I marched over to the chairs on the other side of the room and slumped into the seat in the corner. The floor was stained and dirty. I kicked at a scuff mark. How dare Jam say I was obsessed? Let him try and live not knowing about his past. He'd soon realise how hard it was. Like walking through an earthquake. The ground always shifting under your feet as you imagined one possible history after another.

I bent over, determined Jam shouldn't see me cry.

Silence. Then the cab operator called Jam over to his booth. I could hear them speaking in low voices.

I wiped my eyes. Footsteps. A shadow fell over the scuff mark on the floor. Jam squatted down in front of me.

He leaned towards me, his head tilted sideways, trying to see my face.

'The cab's ready,' he said. He paused. 'D'you really want to go to this Leavington place?'

I nodded, still not trusting myself to look up at him.

Jam put his hand on the chair next to me. 'On your own?' he said.

I gritted my teeth. It was no good. Just the thought of doing all this by myself was enough to turn me into a quivering wreck.

'No,' I sobbed. 'I want you to come.' I looked up at him, a tear trickling down my cheek. 'Please?'

Jam's eyes softened. I'd never noticed but they were hazel, not brown. With gold flecks beside the green.

I looked away quickly, wiping my face again.

Crap. I must look totally hideous. Just like he said.

Jam squeezed my arm. 'Leavington, then,' he said. 'Bring it on.'

12

Lincoln Heights

Leavington was a dump. So run-down it made Marchfield look smart. Street after street of big apartment buildings all bunched together in straggly lines, with front yards full of rubbish.

The cab driver was massively narked when we explained we wanted to stop off at Lincoln Heights for thirty minutes or so.

He refused to wait for us unless we covered his fare – which would have taken too much of our remaining money.

'It's OK,' I said to Jam. 'We'll get another cab to Burlington. Or a bus.'

Once he knew he wasn't getting his full fare to the airport the driver grumbled the whole way to Leavington. He grumbled about having to look up Lincoln Heights on his map. Then he grumbled about some one-way system which meant he couldn't drop us outside. When he finally did pull up, he made a massive fuss about not having much change and needing us to give him the exact money. Of course I only had the hundred-dollar bill Taylor Tarsen had given me.

The driver took it, then turned away and dug deep into a pouch beside his seat.

'Here,' he growled. He pushed a huge wodge of folded-over notes into my hand and drove off.

I shoved the money into my pocket and shouldered my bag. It was 6.15 am, just starting to get light. A small knot of older teenagers were leaning against a nearby wall. They looked like they'd been out all night. Two of the guys stared at us, their eyes all hard and threatening.

Heart pounding, I grabbed Jam's arm and strode off in the opposite direction. The weather matched the scenery. Dull, ugly, steel-grey clouds filled every centimetre of sky. And the air was bitterly cold.

Jam spent his last few dollars on weak coffee and dough-nuts from a grubby stall on the corner. Then suddenly we were there. 10904 Lincoln Heights.

It was like all the other buildings in the road. Dark. Dirty. Crumbling. The front door was locked. And none of the buzzers on the chipped side panel appeared to work.

At last a woman came out and scurried down the steps. We slipped inside before the front door shut.

'Ugh.' Jam wrinkled his nose.

I swallowed, trying not to breathe in the rank smell of stale piss and rotting food that drifted down from the stained, concrete stairs.

We made our way slowly up to apartment thirty-four on

the top floor. Once again, I knew that if Jam wasn't beside me I would have turned and run away. In fact, if I hadn't made so much fuss about coming here, I probably would have suggested we left right now.

Surely it was hopeless? There was no way Sonia still lived here. *Jeez.* She'd probably never lived here. I just didn't know. But as we stood outside apartment thirty-four I suddenly had this overwhelming sense she was going to open the door. And then what?

What would I say?

Hey. Did you kidnap me eleven years ago?

Suppose I was wrong? Suppose she really was my mother? Suppose she took one look at me and slammed the door in my face?

Jam was already knocking.

I stood frozen to the spot. The door was opening.

I stared at the girl standing in front of us. Then I relaxed. It wasn't Sonia. Couldn't be Sonia. She was way too young. No more than eighteen or nineteen.

The girl had a baby in her arms, and a toddler clutching at her knee. She tucked a wisp of greasy hair behind her ears and scowled at me.

'What you want?' she said, her voice heavily accented. Spanish, I think.

'We're looking for someone called Sonia Holtwood,' I said. 'I think she used to live here.'

‘No,’ the girl said. ‘She no live here.’ She started closing the door.

‘Wait,’ I said, pushing it open against her.

‘Hey. Dejame. Puta. Get out.’ The girl’s voice rose in a shriek.

‘Please, is there anyone else you can ask? Someone who might remember who used to live here?’

But the girl had totally lost it. She was screaming at me now. Lots of Spanish words I didn’t understand.

‘No se,’ she shouted. ‘I don’t know.’ She slammed the door shut.

I blinked. I could sense a few of the other doors open further down the corridor. People nosing outside to see what all the noise was about. There was a shuffling of feet as they turned and went inside.

I looked up at Jam.

‘Guess that’s it,’ he said.

‘Excuse me, darlin’.’

I looked round. An old lady in the apartment opposite had appeared at her door. She was stooped over with age, and the skin on her face and arms was wrinkled in folds like fine paper.

‘Did I hear you askin’ for Sonia?’ she said ‘Sonia Holtwood?’

‘Yes.’ I looked at her eagerly. ‘Do you know her? Did she used to live here?’

The old lady stared at me with bright, hard eyes. 'Oh yes,' she said. 'She was only here a short time, but I used to babysit her little girl.'

13

Bettina

The lady said her name was Bettina.

'How d'ya'all know Sonia, then?' she said.

'It's not . . . I mean . . .' I stammered, reluctant to tell a stranger my story.

But Bettina guessed. 'You're never Sonia's little girl?' she said.

I nodded, my face flushing.

Bettina clasped her crooked twig-fingers together in delight. 'Saints alive! I never thought . . . Well come in, come in.'

She ushered us into her little apartment, chattering like a bird. 'So where's your mama? Where'd'y'all get that accent?'

I sat on the edge of a fussily patterned chair. It clashed with the carpet and the curtains. The sort of thing Mum hated.

'I was adopted when I was three,' I said awkwardly. 'I live in Britain. I'm trying to find out about Sonia because, because . . .' My voice died away. Apart from the sound of a ticking clock the room was silent.

Because she knows where I'm from. She knows where I belong. Because I think she stole me from my real family.

Bettina stared at me with sad eyes. 'Adopted? Poor child,' she whispered.

I looked round, embarrassed by her sympathy. There were cushions on the seats and little ornaments on every shelf. It was kind of homey. I wondered if I'd ever crawled over the sofa when I was little.

Bettina went off to make some tea. A few minutes later she came back in, a tray of cups and saucers rattling in her hands. Jam jumped up and dashed over to her. 'Let me take that,' he smiled. He set the tray on a low table in front of one of the sofas.

'Charmin',' Bettina nodded approvingly at him. 'What lovely British manners.' She sat down on the sofa.

'When did you last see her?' I said.

Bettina leaned forward and slowly arranged the cups on the saucers. 'She only stayed here a few weeks. An' it was a long, long time ago. Ten, eleven years maybe. People do that now. Come an' go. No roots.'

'So . . . so what was she like?' I said.

Bettina looked down. I noticed her ears were pierced. The long earring was dragging the hole in her earlobe down.

'Sonia was very private,' she said slowly. 'She didn't want people knowin' her business. I prob'ly wouldn't even remember her if it wasn't for you. She never told me anythin' about herself. To be truthful an' all – I hope you don't mind me sayin' – she didn't seem the motherly type.'

Bettina poured the tea, then set the teapot down with a sigh. 'I didn't see much kissin' and cuddlin'.'

I sipped at my tea, my heart beating fast. 'When she left, d'you know where she went?'

Bettina shook her head sorrowfully. 'Darlin' I wish I could tell you. But one day she just upped and left with you. Not a word to anyone.'

'Oh.' I stared into my teacup. A longing filled me. This old lady had known me longer than anyone. Before Mum and Dad, even. 'What was I like?' I spoke before I'd realised I was going to. My voice sounded small.

Bettina put her gnarled hand over mine. 'The cutest little thing,' she said. 'Though I only minded you a few times I'll never forget you. You were real quiet, real serious. Hardly said a word. And you had this sad little face. It took some doing to make you smile. But when you did you were so pretty. There was this one time I sorely wanted to take a picture of you. You were sitting right where you are now.'

'Did you?' I said. 'I mean, do you have the photo?'

Bettina shook her head. 'Sonia came back from wherever she'd been and found me. She was real mad. Pulled the film out of my camera. She moved out the next day.'

We finished our tea and left. Bettina wasn't in any hurry to say goodbye. I got the strong impression that she didn't have many visitors.

Out on the street it was light, but still freezing. I wished for the tenth time since arriving in America that I had brought a warmer jacket.

'Guess we'd better find out about buses to Burlington?' Jam looked at me sideways. I could see he was wondering if I was going to insist we kept trying to find Sonia.

But the trail was cold. There was nothing more I could do. What Bettina had said made me certain that Sonia was not my real mother. Yet I still knew nothing about my life before she found me.

The next logical step was to call the *Missing-Children.com* hotline and tell them I thought I might be Martha Lauren Purditt.

But I didn't want to do that any more than I had wanted to do it back in London. *It's* my *past. I don't want police and officials and Social Services people taking over. Making all the decisions.*

Jam stood there, shivering. He was still looking expectantly at me.

'Let's go into a shop. Ask where the bus station is,' I said.

As we walked down the road towards a convenience

store, I pulled the wodge of dollars out of my pocket. 'How much d'you think . . . ?'

I stared at the unfolding roll of money in my hand. Apart from the dollar bill on top, the other notes were all just plain pieces of grey paper.

'That cab driver,' I hissed.

'What?' Jam looked round.

'He ripped us off with the change for the fare.' My voice rose to a squeak as I rifled desperately through the pieces of paper.

I looked up at Jam.

We had one dollar left.

14

The ride

We walked, unspeaking, towards a small square patch of green between two of the apartment buildings. My ears stung with cold, but I hardly noticed.

We had no money. How were we going to get back to Burlington?

Jam paced up and down on the hard grass. 'We'll just have to ring your mum,' he said.

My heart sank. I knew we had to make the call. But it felt like defeat. The wind whipped round my shoulders. I dragged my jacket round me more tightly. There was no other choice. I dug into my pocket for my mobile.

'You guys need a ride?' I looked round. A middle-aged woman with wavy brown hair was leaning out of a car window, smiling at us.

Instinctively I shook my head and turned away. The woman opened her car door and leaned further out. She was wearing a police uniform. 'Hey, I don't bite,' she laughed. 'Where you folks headed?'

I caught Jam's eye. We walked over to the woman together.

She was older than she looked from a distance. Her hair was very set. It might even have been a wig. And she wore heavy blue eye make-up and loads of face powder.

'I just spotted you guys out here. You look cold.' The woman glanced up into the cloudy sky. 'Weather forecast reckons it'll snow later,' she said.

The woman reached into her jacket and pulled out a leather wallet. She flipped it open and flashed it front of us. I caught a glimpse of a star-shaped badge and the words *Police Dept*. 'I'm Suzanna Sanders,' the woman smiled. 'On vacation as from my last shift. You guys sure I can't drop you anywhere?'

I chewed my lip. 'We're going to Burlington, then Boston. The airports.' I said.

Suzanna Sanders's eyes widened. 'No way. I'm going to Boston, too. Flight from Logan.' She looked down at her uniform. 'I'm on a tight schedule as you can see. I'm gonna have to change at the airport. So make up your minds.'

'Can you wait a minute?' I said. 'I just want to talk to my friend.'

I pulled Jam away from the car. 'I think we should go with her.'

'What, get in a total stranger's car?'

'She's a police officer,' I said. 'She's not going to hurt us.'

'Suppose your mum's called the police?' Jam said. 'They might be looking for us.'

'So? We're going back to Mum anyway. This way we get to Boston quicker than we would if we had to go back to Burlington first.' I glanced at Suzanna Sanders. 'If she asks, we can say we got lost or something. And we're trying to get back to Mum in Boston. I'll text Mum now, tell her that's where we're going.'

'I'm not sure,' Jam said. 'I've got a bad feeling.'

I squeezed his arm. 'Come on, what can happen? She's a cop. And there are two of us.'

Jam nodded. 'OK.'

I turned back to the policewoman and told her our names. 'Thanks. If it's really all right, we will come with you. I just have to text my mum.'

'Great,' Suzanna smiled. 'But would you mind texting in the car? I'm freezing my ass off out here.'

I followed her over to her car. I hesitated, not wanting to sit alone in the front with her, but also not wanting to force Jam to either.

'It's OK, you guys take the back seat.' Suzanna opened the door. 'But no smooching.'

I blushed as I got inside. Suzanna put our backpacks in the boot as we slid along the leatherette seat. The car inside was as smart and polished as it was outside. I rubbed my frozen hands together, then pulled my phone out and switched it on. Yet more missed calls and messages. I ignored them and punched in Mum's number. Nothing. I checked the battery – still half-full. Then I noticed I had no signal.

Jam checked his as the car drew off. Same thing.

'Often happens round here,' Suzanna said cheerfully. Give it five minutes then try again.'

Jam settled wearily against the opposite window. He pulled his PSP out of his jacket pocket and switched it on. But he didn't play it. He turned it over and rubbed his thumb over the neat gouges on the back – the six stripes I'd noticed in the motel.

'What are they for?' I said.

'Nothing.' Jam shrugged. He gazed out the window as we roared past a row of flat-roofed shops.

I tried my phone several more times, but still couldn't get a signal. I left it switched on.

'You guys want some juice?' Suzanna reached onto the passenger seat and passed a couple of orange-juice cartons back to us. We gulped them down thirstily.

To my relief, Suzanna didn't ask us any questions about where we came from or why we were in Leavington. I leaned my head against the damp chill of the car window. After a few minutes I began to feel sleepy. I looked over at Jam. His eyes were shut, his head lolling against the seat behind him.

I felt my own head nodding.

I was back on the beach. Alone. Scared. I reached the

rock where I had seen the flash of long black hair. No one was there. I turned round, suddenly full of panic. 'Mommy,' I wailed. 'Mommeeeee. Where are you?'

When I woke up it was dark outside. The car was humming along a deserted road. No street lights, but a white glow shone off the ground. I sat up, feeling groggy.

Jam was still asleep.

'No.' Suzanna's voice was low and angry. It took me a second to realise she was speaking into her cellphone. 'Don't order me around, Taylor,' she spat. 'It's your fault we're in this mess. An' yet look who's the one clearing it up.'

She threw the phone onto the passenger seat beside her.

My head felt like a big cotton-wool ball. Taylor. There was something significant about that name. Something I should remember.

'Where are we?' I rubbed my forehead.

Suzanna rolled back her shoulders. 'Nearly there,' she said. 'Hey, guess what? I was right – it did snow. You guys have been asleep for hours.'

I shivered. There was something about the way Suzanna spoke – a hard edge to her voice – that hadn't been there before. I reached for the phone in my jeans pocket.

It wasn't there.

Maybe it had fallen on the floor. I reached down and groped along the floor of the car. As I reached where Jam was sitting I tugged at his leg. 'Jam, wake up. I can't find my phone.'

Jam yawned and stretched his arms.

'It's not here,' I said.

'Must be,' Suzanna said from the front seat. She coughed. 'We're nearly at Logan. I'll put the light on when we get there. We can have a proper look.'

I sat back in my seat, feeling uneasy. I was sure my phone had been in my pocket before I went to sleep. How could it have just fallen out?

Come to that, how could it be dark now? I checked my watch – 7 pm. I forced my fuggy brain to think. It couldn't have been later than nine this morning that we left Bettina's. How could we have been asleep for over ten hours? And surely we should have been in Boston long before now?

I looked out of the window, straining to see a road sign.

Nothing. Just snow and trees on either side. It didn't even look as if we were on a proper, made-up road.

I slid along the leatherette seat and leaned my head against Jam's shoulder. His whole body tensed.

I flicked my eyes over to the central mirror. Suzanna was staring at me. She raised her eyebrows, then looked back at the road ahead. I tilted my head upward, towards Jam's neck.

I could feel him pulling away from me. 'What are you . . . ?'

'Sssh.' My lips found Jam's ear. 'I think Suzanna took my phone,' I whispered. 'And I don't think we're anywhere near Logan Airport.'

Jam's breath was hot on my cheek. He drew back, fumbling in his own pocket. Then he leaned forward again and whispered. 'Mine's gone too. As soon as she stops the car, we get out, OK?'

'Hey, lovebirds, cut it out,' Suzanna said. 'I don't wanna get pulled over.' She gave a hollow laugh.

I moved back to the other side of the back seat. But I reached out my fingers and found Jam's hand. Our fingers twisted round each other. My heart was hammering against my throat.

'I don't feel well,' I said. 'Can you stop the car?'

Suzanna ignored me.

Although the car was moving, it was slower now, rattling over the lumps and bumps of the unmade track. I reached for the door handle. I had some mad idea Jam and I could jump out of the car. But the door was locked. I could hear Jam fumbling with the handle on the other side.

Suzanna twisted half round in her seat. 'Cut it out.'

'What are you doing?' My voice rose with panic. 'Where are you taking us?'

Oh God, oh God. She's a psycho. Like the sort who Mum says kills two kids a year. And Jam and I are this year's two kids.

Suzanna looked at me in her rearview mirror.

'Don't you recognise me, sweetie?' She grinned nastily and put on a fake, sugar-sweet voice. 'I'm Sonia Holtwood.'

15

No escape

I stared stupidly at the back of her head, at her neat, set, brown hair. She was Sonia Holtwood?

My mind was too dazed to make sense of it.

'What do you mean?' I said.

'Taylor told me you've been asking questions. Trying to find me,' the woman said, evenly. 'I decided I'd better find you first.'

I frowned, still struggling to get my head round what was happening. Taylor, again. Where had I heard that name recently? Then I remembered. It was Mr Tarsen's first name.

'Mr Tarsen called you?' I said.

'Correct.' The woman flicked on the car floodlights. 'He said it was obvious you knew more than you were saying. Not that he *did* anything. No, he just turned off the burglar alarm, hid your file – waited to see what *you* did. Typical freakin' Taylor.'

My mind seemed to have crashed like an overloaded computer. I stared out of the window. A dense pine forest was all around us. Snow was falling.

'But you're a police officer,' Jam insisted. 'We saw your badge.'

'Costume rental.' I could hear the smug grin in Sonia Holtwood's voice. 'That's the great thing about tourists. They think they know what cops look like but they've only ever seen them on TV shows. If you hadn't got in the car I'd have arrested you.' She laughed. 'So you guys feeling OK?'

Suddenly it all fell into place. 'You drugged us,' I said. 'The orange juice. You took our phones.'

I caught Jam's eye. His face was ghostly pale in the reflected light from the snow-covered trees outside.

'What do you want?' My voice trembled. 'What are you going to do with us?'

Sonia ignored me. She drove on for half a minute or so more, then pulled the car over to the side of the track. She switched off the ignition but kept the headlamps on.

Fear flooded through me like ice water. I reached for the door handle and pulled. It was still locked.

Sonia turned round and stared at us both.

'You've got no idea what it's like to have nothing,' she said. 'No money. No hope. No future.'

I wrestled with the handle, panic twisting and slicing at my throat. 'Let us out,' I shouted.

'You were a spoilt little princess when you were three as well,' Sonia sneered. 'Bright and white and worth a fortune.'

I turned on her, fury suddenly swamping my fear. 'You stole me from my family. You—'

'I was in debt,' Sonia spat. 'I needed the money.'

'You evil piece of—'

'Shut up.' Sonia reached out and slapped my face.

'Hey!' Jam yelled.

I gasped at the sudden pain. My hand flew to my cheek. I slumped back into my seat.

Jam reached out for my hand again.

I stared at Sonia's hard, angry face. Beyond her, through the windscreen, white snowflakes fluttered yellow in the light from the car's headlamps.

'When Taylor called,' she said, 'I could have just turned and run. Taken the risk that the Feds would never find me. And then I thought – why should *I* run? Why should *I* hide? So I followed you from that sleazy motel you were staying in.'

Her eyes were like black holes. Dead. Empty.

I suddenly realised why Mr Tarsen hadn't come after us himself or called the police when we broke into the agency. He knew we could be traced to Marchfield. To him. He didn't want anyone else looking for us. Only Sonia.

'We won't tell anyone what you did,' I pleaded. 'I promise.'

Sonia raised her eyebrows. 'Oh?'

She pressed a button on the dashboard. With a click,

both back doors unlocked. I wrenched my door open and hurled myself outside, slamming the door shut behind me. A whirl of icy wind whipped round me like a snake. I turned. Jam was outside the car too. Sonia was twisting round, reaching into the back of the car, pulling his door shut.

The night air here was far colder than in Marchfield. It was like being inside a freezer.

Sonia revved up the car engine. I realised with a jolt exactly what she was planning.

'No!' Jam shouted.

I tugged at my door handle. Locked. 'Wait,' I cried.

Sonia grinned. She wound down her window a couple of centimetres.

'Thought you wanted out?' she said.

'Where are we?' Jam yelled.

'Middle of nowhere,' she said. 'Twenty miles from anywhere with a name.'

My heart hammered as I stared at her. Snow whirled in my face. I was colder than I'd ever been in my life. I hugged my thin jacket round me. I might as well not have been wearing it.

Sonia started edging the car backwards.

'You can't leave us here,' Jam yelled, running alongside the car.

Seeing the terror in his face was like a trigger. Instantly

my whole body started shaking. 'We'll freeze to death,' I cried.

Sonia scowled up at us. 'No shit.' She turned the car across the track.

'At least leave us our stuff,' Jam shouted. 'Our phones.'

But Sonia simply closed the car window and spun the wheels round so she was facing back down the track.

'She can't do this,' I said.

But she had.

The car crunched over the snow, then slowly disappeared into the darkness. Its two rear lights glowed in the distance, like the golden eyes of a giant cat. Then they, too, vanished into the night.

The wind bit into my face. Snow was still falling. I hugged my frozen hands under my armpits and stared at the ground. Snow was already covering the tracks the car had made.

In that moment I realised just how brilliant Sonia and Tarsen's plan was. No one had seen us get into Sonia's car. No one could link us being here to either of them. In fact no one even knew we *were* here. Which meant no one was even looking for us.

I stared down at my trainers, aware that I couldn't feel my feet. The tips of the white leather were stained dark from the snow.

'We have to keep moving,' Jam said beside me. He was

feeling in his pockets. 'Have you got anything on you? Anything at all?'

I shook my head. Jam pulled his PSP out of his jacket pocket. He looked at me, his eyes angry and hard.

'Don't suppose we can turn that into anything useful?' I said, my teeth chattering.

'Seeing as I'm not Alex Rider, no,' Jam snapped.

We set off down the track. Snowflakes fell on my nose and cheeks and hair. A drop on my neck melted and trickled coldly down my back.

I was shivering uncontrollably now. I glanced sideways at Jam. 'How far d'you think it is, back to the road?'

He shrugged. 'Miles. But the track bent round. I think we should go through the trees. It might cut off some of the track, save time.'

'Suppose a car comes, though. Shouldn't we stay on the track?'

Jam stared at me. 'There won't be a car.' His voice was scathing. 'That's why she left us here.'

He turned and walked into the trees on the left.

I hurried after him, my feet silent in the thick snow. My heart beat fast under my ribs. I could taste the fear in my throat. What was going to happen to us? Jam stomped beside me, not looking at me at all.

Why was he acting like this was my fault? I watched my breath steaming out of my mouth in a thick white cloud.

We walked on for what felt like miles. The pine trees grew closer together, the snow deeper and icier. My arms and legs were stiff and numb. Somewhere in the distance an animal howled.

'D'you think there are wolves here?' I said.

'Yeah, and bears – but don't worry, the cold will probably get us before the wild animals,' Jam said, sarcastically. He tugged his PSP out of his pocket and ran his finger over the grooves on the back.

I forced my frozen feet to move. My cotton jumper was soaked from the falling snow. It clung like a thick, damp skin against my body.

'Come on,' Jam snapped. 'We need to go faster.'

I bit my lip. 'Why are you so angry with me?' I said.

Jam spun round. His face was suddenly contorted with rage. His voice echoed above the icy wind.

'You are unbelievable, Lauren!' he shouted. 'It's always, always, about you, isn't it? You are the most self-obsessed person I've ever met.'

My throat tightened. 'What d'you mean?'

Jam flung out his hand, knocking a line of snow off a branch.

'Don't you get it?' He pointed towards the trees and the sky. 'We're in the middle of nowhere. We're going to die from the cold. And you think I'm angry with you?'

'I didn't mean—'

'No, course you didn't. Just like you didn't mean to drag me halfway round the world and force me into a car with a homicidal maniac.'

'I didn't force you—'

'No you asked me, and I said yes, which makes me even more stupid than you are selfish,' Jam spat.

I stared at him, my whole body trembling with fear and cold and shock. 'Jam—' I started.

'No.' Jam turned and strode away into the trees. I tried to follow him, but my legs were shaking too much. I stumbled and fell onto the snow.

I sat up, sobbing. 'Jam,' I called out. 'I'm sorry.'

Silence.

I looked around me. The only light came from the cloudy sky and the white of the snow around me. I was surrounded by pine trees.

There was no sign of Jam. Tears streamed down my face. I tried to push myself up, but my limbs ached too much. I felt lightheaded. My breath was coming in shallow gasps.

I was alone. Fear swallowed me – a dark hole inside my heart where I was nothing. No one.

I slid down onto the ground, expecting it to feel hard and cold. But it didn't. The snow was soft and warm, like a blanket. I lay stretched out in it, overcome by a delicious feeling of drowsiness. Sleep was all I wanted.

It would take me to the woman on the beach. It would take me home.

I closed my eyes and sank down into the darkness.

16

Glane

In the distance I could hear voices. Someone was calling my name. Something hot and wet seeped between my lips and trickled down my chin. Tea. Sweet tea.

I spluttered. I hate sugar in my tea.

'Is she all right?' It was Jam's voice. I struggled to open my eyes, but my eyelids were too heavy.

A large, calloused hand pressed down on my forehead. 'Let her sleep,' said a gruff, gentle voice.

I knew there was a question I wanted to ask, but I was too tired to think what it was, let alone open my mouth and speak. I turned over. Some kind of blanket – soft and furry – tickled at my chin. I arched my neck and nestled down again.

I was running towards the big rock. I heard laughing on the other side. I crept up, stepping carefully across the sand. I peered round the rock. There she was, her back turned. Her long black hair tumbled down to her waist. It was shiny and soft. I reached up and stroked it.

She turned around. She smiled. And, at last, I saw her

face. She was young. Full of life, with the kindest, bluest eyes I'd ever seen. I gasped. She was beautiful – like an angel.

'Little one,' she said. 'You found me.'

Later, much later, I woke up disoriented. An orange light glowed through my closed eyelids. My face was warm. I moved my arms and legs. They felt weak, but not hurt.

I opened my eyes.

I was in some kind of wooden cabin. It was sparse, but scrubbed clean. A table and two chairs stood in one corner next to a large cupboard. A huge fire crackled in the fireplace opposite, next to a heap of roughly chopped logs.

One wall was lined with shelves covered with books. Jam was curled up on a cushion on the floor beneath the shelves, reading. A strand of hair fell over his eyes, almost touching his nose.

He must have sensed me looking at him because he looked up. His face broke into a huge smile.

'Lauren,' he said. 'How d'you feel?'

I struggled onto my elbows. 'Hungry,' I said. 'Where are we?'

'North Vermont – Cold Ridge National Forest.' Jam darted over to the fire and tore at a loaf of bread laid out on a cloth beside the fireplace. 'This is Glane's place.' Jam brought a chunk back for me, then fetched some water from a jug by the door.

'Who's Glane?' As I sipped the water I looked round the room again. There was a row of beautiful wood carvings along the window ledge. Graceful ovals and wave-shapes and circles with holes in.

'You'll see,' Jam said. 'He'll be back soon. He found us.'

'Found us?' I said.

Jam nodded. 'In the wood.' His face coloured. 'He found me first. I . . . Oh, Lauren, I'm so, so sorry I ran off . . .'

I shrugged, unsure what to say. In the first few moments after waking I'd forgotten about Jam leaving me in the snow. Now it flooded back, along with everything else. Sonia Holtwood. Knowing for sure that she'd kidnapped me when I was a little girl. And my mother's angel face.

Jam's blush deepened. 'You gotta know, though. I didn't really go anywhere. I mean, I just stomped off for a minute. I knew where you were . . .'

The cabin door swung open, letting in a brilliant stream of cold air and sharp sunlight. For a second I could see blue sky and snow stretching away from the door, then a huge figure completely wrapped in furs and fleeces, a rifle slung over his shoulder, appeared in the doorway.

The figure stamped its boots outside, then strode indoors.

'This is Glane,' Jam said. There was a note of pride in his voice, almost as if he was showing the man off to me.

Glane pulled off his hat and gloves. Above a bushy beard, his face was lined and leathery. It was impossible to tell how old he was. His eyes twinkled deep and brown as he reached forward to shake my hand.

'Hey, Lauren. How you doing?' His accent was American but tinged with a slightly singsong twang.

I swung my legs off the bed, placing my feet on a faded rug on the floor. 'I'm good,' I said.

It wasn't rational to be nervous. The guy had saved our lives. But what was he doing here in the middle of nowhere? I mean, did he live out here like some kind of weirdo hermit?

Glane looked at me. It made me feel uncomfortable, as if he could see what I was thinking.

'Now Lauren's up I guess we'll have to go,' Jam said. He sounded slightly reluctant.

'How long was I asleep?' I said.

'All last night, Sunday, and most of the day today.' Glane grinned. 'It's too late to go anywhere now. But if it is not snowing tomorrow morning, we will set off then.'

I glanced at Jam. 'Did you call Mum?'

He shook his head. 'There's no phone here.'

'You're kidding?' I said, shocked.

Glane's laugh was like a rumble of thunder. 'No phone. No electricity. No modern conveniences of any kind.'

I looked round the room again. It was certainly spartan. And yet there were soft touches too – the wood carvings, a tawny-coloured curtain at the window and a bowl of pine cones on the table. 'But we need to get back,' I said.

I guess I should have been thinking about Mum and Dad and how worried they'd be now. And part of me was certainly worrying about Sonia Holtwood – scared she would somehow realise we had been rescued and come after us again.

Yes. All those feelings were there, like background noise in my head. But they faded beside the image of my mother – the beautiful woman on the beach. Now I'd seen her face – now Sonia had admitted she stole me – nothing was going to stop me finding her as soon as I got out of these woods.

'There is no problem.' Glane sat down at the table. 'The nearest town from here is Wells Canyon. About twenty miles away. We should be able to cover it in a day – but you'll have to borrow my spare boots. Yours are split.' I followed his glance over to the corner where my trainers lay on their sides. Even from the bed I could see the cracks in the soles.

Glane stood up, his huge frame dominating the small room. I stared at his enormous feet.

'I don't think your boots will fit me,' I stammered.

Glane laughed – a rich, low, belly laugh. 'No. So I will make a lining for you. Tonight.' He turned to Jam. 'I have killed a couple of rabbits outside. Will you help me skin them?'

Ugh. *A weirdo hermit rabbit butcher.*

I looked at Jam, expecting to see him making a disgusted face. But, astonishingly, Jam had already leaped to his feet and was halfway to the door.

He had to be kidding? Take the skin off an animal? How gross was that?

'Lauren?' Glane smiled at me. 'D'you want to help?'

I shook my head. *Do you want me to hurl?*

'Bet you enjoy eating them though,' Glane grinned.

I blinked.

'You rest up,' Glane continued. 'Put another log on the fire if you like. And you are welcome to look around.'

He and Jam disappeared outside. I explored the cabin. In one of the large cupboards was some dry food and a stack of plates and mugs. In the other were three violins with parts of their wooden panelling missing. The books were a strange mix. Lots of hardbacks full of stiff, glossy pictures of ancient musical instruments. And a row of flimsy manuals with titles like *How to Pluck a Chicken* and *Basic Outdoor Cookery.*

Who was this guy?

Glane came back in just as I was tearing off another hunk of bread. I stepped back guiltily.

'Eat,' he said. 'It is OK.' He picked up a large wooden bucket and turned to go back outside.

'How long have you lived here?' I said.

Glane grinned. 'I do not live here. I just come for a month each year. I was going back home today. Back to Boston.'

I tried to imagine him in a busy, bustling city.

'You live in Boston?'

Glane nodded. 'I have a job. Repairing musical instruments.'

I watched him stride across the snow to where Jam was waiting beside a tree stump. The sun glinted on a massive axe at his feet. Glane picked it up like it was a toy and swung it behind his head. He was obviously showing Jam how to use it.

Great. A weirdo hermit butcher violin-mender with an axe.

Jam took the axe and copied Glane's swing. Up, up in the air, then thud. The axe slammed down into the tree stump.

'Very back-to-nature,' I muttered. I took a deep breath and sighed it out.

Jam walked over to a snow drift. Glane gave him the bucket he'd taken from the cabin and pointed at a patch of snow. I pulled on my cracked trainers and went outside. The sun was low in the sky, but warm on the back of my head.

Jam's face was glowing with delight as I strolled up.

'Glane's showing me which bits of snow to take to melt for water,' he said.

I wanted to laugh.

Oh, great. That'll come in handy when we get back to north London.

But Jam looked so excited and pleased with himself that I said nothing.

After a couple more minutes I could feel the snow seeping in through the cracks in my shoes. I trudged back to the cabin.

My mother's face was still in my head. A stronger presence than the woods and the snow. Stronger even than Jam.

I sat by the fire and stared into the flames. If I could only find her, then everything else in my life would make sense.

I would know who I was, at last.

17

More real than real life

Darkness fell. Glane lit two lanterns, then cooked a stew with the rabbit meat and some herbs. It smelled delicious, but the thought of eating it after knowing the others had skinned the rabbits made me feel slightly sick.

Jam smacked his lips. 'Awesome.'

'Really?' I said.

Jam's mouth stretched into this wide grin. 'Try it.'

Tentatively, I sipped a spoonful of the meat sauce. It was good. And I was hungry.

I tucked in.

After we'd eaten, Glane took the dishes outside. I didn't think I was tired, but when I lay down on the bed I drifted into this warm, comfy sleep.

She was there again. My mother. Her face full of love for me. She bent over me. She gently stroked my cheek. Her finger was soft and warm. Just the lightest touch.

My heart leaped. It was real. She was there. It was really happening.

I strained, trying to swim up out of my sleep.

I forced my eyes to open.

No one was there. I looked round. The cabin was empty, except for Jam standing a couple of metres away looking at one of Glane's books. He was frowning at the page, clearly completely engrossed in what he was reading.

I lay back, letting the waves of loss flow through me.

Glane stomped inside, bringing with him a blast of icy air. He strode over to the fire and sat down.

'Time to make your boot lining,' he said. 'Want to help, Lauren?'

I didn't see how I could refuse.

For one horrible second I thought he might be planning to use the rabbit skins from earlier.

Then he rummaged in a basket on the floor and drew out some lengths of fleece. I sighed with relief.

Glane wrapped the material round my foot, then measured it against a pair of walking boots. I helped him cut and stitch the fleece. Soon it began to take a rough boot-shape.

Jam still hadn't looked up from his book.

'Doesn't Jam need boot linings too?' I said.

'His boots did not fall apart,' Glane said.

I shifted uncomfortably in my chair. How did Glane

manage to make everything he said sound like the end of a conversation?

Jam finally put down his book. He walked to the door.

'I'm going outside,' he grinned. 'For another freeze-ya-butt-outdoor-peeing experience.'

As he shut the door behind him, it struck me that Jam was actually enjoying being here. He certainly felt more comfortable around Glane than I did.

A twinge of jealousy twisted in my stomach. I wasn't used to sharing Jam with anyone.

I wandered over to look at the book he had been reading, one of the flimsy manuals: *Making Fire Without Matches.*

For God's sake.

Glane had put down the boot lining and was gazing at me. My heart thudded. *Here it comes. Weirdo hermit axe-murderer attacks defenceless teen in deserted wood cabin.*

'So you are searching for your past?' Glane said matter-of-factly.

I stared at him, shocked. 'Jam told you?'

Glane nodded. 'Of course. Do you not think I asked why you were here in the woods dying of the cold?'

I turned away. It was my secret. My story. Jam had had no right.

'Don't be angry,' Glane said softly. 'He thought you were going to die. He was very frightened. Very upset. Ashamed that he had lost his temper, run away.'

I looked up. 'He told you about that too?'

Glane nodded, turning back to the fleece. His fingers were like great, fat sausages, yet they moved deftly over the material. 'We talked for a long time about it while you slept. We agreed it is not what a man does.'

I shook my head, my irritation with Jam turning into annoyance with Glane. OK, so maybe the guy wasn't an axe-murderer, but he was definitely an insufferably pompous jerk-head.

'I don't see what being a man's got to do with it,' I snapped. 'Anyway, Jam's only fifteen. Not exactly a man.'

'He is trying to become one,' Glane said. He tugged at the stitched fleece, testing to see if it held. 'It's not as easy as you think. Especially without a father to guide you. Here. Your linings are finished.'

He handed them to me. They looked like thick, furry socks.

'Jam *has* a father,' I said. 'His parents are divorced, not dead. It's me who's lost my parents.'

Glane moved the lantern closer and started tidying away scraps of fleece.

The words were out of my mouth before I realised I was going to say them.

'I've seen her face,' I said. 'In my memories. My real mum. I found her. I mean . . . in my dream. But I know she's there, waiting for me.'

I stopped. What was I doing? My memories were private, secret, fragile. And here I was, blabbing about them to this weird guy I'd only just met.

Glane stared at me. 'But Lauren,' he said. 'This is all only inside your head. It is not real.'

I pulled on the boot linings.

Glane didn't understand. How could he? It's impossible to explain what it feels like, when something inside your head is more real than your real life.

18

Out of the woods

We left very early the next morning. A few snowflakes whirled down from a cloudy sky, but Glane was confident there wouldn't be a storm. He loaned us jumpers and hats and gloves.

The fleece linings Glane had made padded out his enormous walking boots well, but they still felt big and heavy on my feet. My legs ached by the time we stopped for a brief meal of bread (baked in the cabin fire in a sealed tin the night before) and water (fresh melted snow – boiled then cooled).

We walked and walked, past endless trees and along snow-covered tracks. Glane never looked once at a map, but he seemed to know exactly where he was going the whole time.

It was almost dark when we arrived at Wells Canyon Lodge, on the outskirts of what Glane said was a small town about two hundred miles east of Burlington. My legs were totally exhausted and my eyes were sore from the sun and snow.

Glane booked us all in and we went upstairs. As Jam and I trudged along the corridor to our rooms, my stomach churned. I dreaded calling Mum. She would be mad enough with me for running off. How on earth was I going to get her to understand how much I needed to find my real mother?

Jam looked pretty anxious too. He went into his room without saying anything. Mine was a few doors down. Bare, but clean. I smoothed my hand over the nubby cotton counterpane. A large, old-fashioned white phone stood beside the bed. I stared at it.

It took me five minutes to work up the courage to dial Mum's mobile number.

'Hello?' A voice like a wound-up spring.

'Mum?'

'Lauren.' The voice almost collapsed in on itself. 'Are you all right? Are you safe?'

'I'm OK, Mum, everything's fine.'

'Oh my God, Lauren.' Mum dissolved into tears.

I sat on the edge of the bed. 'I'm sorry, Mum.'

'Where *are* you?'

I told her. But when I tried to explain what had happened, she just kept asking over and over if I was really all right.

'We're still in Boston, but we can be with you in a few hours,' she said. 'Dad's here too. And the FBI. They tracked you to Burlington, but no one remembered you after that.

You'll have to talk to them about who took you from the airport, but—'

I sat up, my heart thudding. What was she talking about? 'Wait. Mum. Listen. Back at Logan Airport – we left on . . . on purpose. It was me. I got Jam to do it. But I had to find out. About where I come from.'

Shocked silence.

'What?' Mum gasped.

'You wouldn't talk about it so I . . . we went to Marchfield. I—'

'I thought you'd been abducted by some lunatic from the airport,' Mum shrieked. 'I thought you were *dead*, Lauren.'

'But I texted to say we were all right,' I stammered. 'I didn't want you to worry. You're always saying how psychos are very rare.'

'Not worry?' Mum shrieked. 'How was I supposed to know someone hadn't *made* you send that text?'

My head flooded with guilt. That possibility hadn't occurred to me.

Mum sucked in her breath. 'So while I've been sitting here unable to sleep or eat for five days solid, you've been gallivanting around America with your boyfriend, trying to find out things which we didn't want to tell you because we thought you weren't old enough. A decision you have just confirmed in its rightness by your absolute selfishness . . .'

‘But . . . look, I’m sorry, Mum.’ I hesitated, trying to work out what to say to make her understand. ‘We were only supposed to be gone for a few hours. Listen. Mum, I . . . I know about Sonia Holtwood and—’

‘You don’t know anything, Lauren.’ Mum’s voice was suddenly harsh and low.

‘Mum, she followed us,’ I pleaded. ‘She tricked us . . . tried to kill us.’ I shivered, remembering how I’d felt in the car and in the woods.

‘You just said you went off on your own.’

‘We did. This was later, after we’d seen Mr Tarsen.’ I stopped. It was hopeless. Everything that had happened was coming out all muddled. None of it mattered now anyway. Only one thing was important. ‘Mum, you have to listen to me. Sonia Holtwood admitted what she did when I was—’

‘ENOUGH.’ Mum’s yell was so loud that I jerked the phone away from my ear.

I sat there, my heart pounding. Slowly I brought the receiver back to my ear. I could hear Mum breathing heavily on the other end. I suddenly remembered what Sonia had said about me being worth ‘a fortune’ when I was little.

Somebody must have paid her that fortune. Why else would she have let me go?

‘Did you buy me from her?’ I whispered. My stomach twisted into a knot. ‘Did you pay her to take me?’

But Mum went into brisk, organised mode. 'No more, Lauren,' she said. 'We're coming to get you. We'll be there in a few hours.'

'But—?'

'We'll talk about it when we get there.'

She hung up.

I sat on the bed, hunched over my knees.

How could they have done it? There was no other explanation. Mum and Dad were evil, evil people who had paid Sonia to steal me away from my real mother.

My beautiful, kind angel mother.

No wonder they had refused to tell me anything about my adoption. I gritted my teeth, hating them with every cell of my body. I didn't need them. I didn't need anyone else.

And that's when it came to me – the only next step possible.

I went down to the Lodge's computer room and logged onto the internet.

19

Going home

An hour later I was back in my room.

I had a bath, then got changed.

Glane had somehow blagged me and Jam some spare clothes from the hotel. Stuff left behind by former staff. Mine was entirely hideous: a pair of outsize green combats, two drainingly grey sweatshirts and a pair of ancient, hot-pink trainers. I tugged the tiny plastic bathroom comb through my hair, wishing I had some hair wax and a nail file. And some make-up. My skin was red raw from the cold and snow and my lips were chapped.

I looked at myself in the mirror.

My heart sank.

This was not how I wanted to look when I found my real mother. She was so beautiful, she'd never believe I was her daughter.

I went down to the Lodge dining room and walked through a sea of empty tables to the one Jam and Glane were sitting at near the bar. A bottle of beer stood on the table in front of Glane, who looked like a different person.

The beard was gone, and he was dressed in dark jeans and a crisp, white T-shirt. He looked up from the menu he was studying as I approached.

'Mmnn.' He licked his lips. 'Buckwheat pancakes with maple syrup for me.'

I sat down. 'Skinned rabbits not available, then?' I said.

Glane smiled. 'No. Anyway, I only eat meat when there is nothing else. And when I've killed it myself.' He glanced sideways at me. 'I don't see why someone else should have to skin my rabbits for me.'

I ignored this and cleared my throat. 'I've got something to tell you.'

'What?' Jam took a long swig of Glane's beer. I noticed he was wearing new clothes too. Much nicer than mine. Jeans and a black jumper. His hair was damp and slicked back from his face.

I hesitated. 'Martha Lauren Purditt went missing in Evanport, near where she was born. It's in Connecticut.'

Jam raised his eyebrows. 'So?'

'I'm going there. Now. I've checked the internet directories. The Purditts – the family who lost her – still live there.'

Jam frowned. 'How d'you know it's the same Purditts?' he said.

'I looked back at the news stories from when . . . from when Martha went missing. Their names are Annie and

Sam Purditt. Bits and pieces of their address are in the different stories.' I sighed. 'I should have done it ages ago, but there was stuff I didn't know then.'

My mother's face. Now I know her face I only have to see her and I'll know if I'm Martha or not.

Glane scratched his freshly shaved chin. 'But your parents? The police?'

I couldn't bring myself to tell him that I was sure Mum and Dad had been involved in kidnapping me in the first place.

'Mum and Dad don't understand how important it is for me to know who I am,' I said, lamely.

A slow smile curled across Glane's mouth. 'This seeking out of your birth family will not tell you who you are. It will only tell you if you are somebody's missing child.'

I shook my head. 'Don't you think the family I was taken from have a right to know what happened to me?'

'Yes, I do. But it will be hard. For everybody. You should wait. Talk to people first.' Glane paused. 'Lauren, I think you see dreams. You are not seeing what is real. What is right under your nose.'

I stood up. 'Right. Anyway, I'm going.'

'How?' Jam cut in. 'How're you gonna get there?' He took another swig of Glane's beer.

I took a deep breath. 'I'm going to hitch-hike.'

Jam spluttered his beer on the tablecloth. 'No way,' he

said angrily. 'I can't believe you'd even consider that after what happened to us.'

'Well, what else can I do?' I looked down, my face burning. 'I just wanted to say thank you for everything you've done. And that I'll pay you both back when I can.'

My hands were shaking as I walked away.

I stood at the hotel entrance, pulling on the second of my two ugly sweatshirts. The highway was a few hundred metres up the road.

My tummy rumbled. I started to wish I'd timed my dramatic exit for after I'd eaten. But even if I left now I probably only had a few hours before Mum and Dad arrived.

'Nobody's going to give you a ride wearing those shoes,' a voice said behind me.

I spun round. Jam was staring at my hot-pink trainers. He looked up. 'You can't do this, Lazerbrain. It's too dangerous.'

'My decision.' I folded my arms and walked outside.

Damn, it was cold.

'Why are you mad at me?' Jam said.

'I'm not,' I said, walking more quickly.

'Then why are you shutting me out like this? And what's with all that poncey "I'll pay you back when I can" crap? I thought we were friends?'

'Really? I thought you were Glane's friend now.' I

winced, even as the words were blurting their way out of my mouth. I knew I sounded childish and stupid.

Jam grabbed my arm to stop me walking any further. He pulled me round to face him. 'Are you jealous?' he grinned.

'Course not.' I glared at him. 'It's just that I know you think I'm obsessed and selfish. I was kind of assuming you wouldn't want to help me any more.'

We were at the very edge of the Lodge's grounds. The lights that marked the start of the highway twinkled up ahead. The place where Jam was holding my arm was the only warm spot on my whole body.

'I do think you're obsessed,' he said, slowly. 'But you're still my friend.'

I stood there, trying not to shiver in the biting night air. I felt a stab of guilt. It *was* mean of me to just walk off when he'd been so brilliant.

Jam let go of me, then took his PSP out of his pocket and rubbed his thumb over the notches in the back.

I hesitated. After all we'd been through, I didn't want to say goodbye to him like this.

'Was your mum angry when you spoke to her?' I said.

'You could say.' Jam rolled his eyes. 'Apparently she told your parents about that stupid hypnotherapy session you had and now they're furious with her for encouraging you. So now she's mad at them. And mad at me for running off. She's out here, you know. Same hotel as your parents. And she's angry about that too, having to leave my sisters with friends.'

'What about your dad?'

'No, he's too busy with his new family.' Jam's face set hard, like a mask. 'Apparently he was going to come over if I didn't turn up after another week or two.'

I frowned. Mum had said my dad had flown to America as soon as I went missing – and I knew how busy he was.

'Another week or two?'

Jam pointed to the six grooves on the back of his PSP. 'D'you remember you asked me about these?' His voice was low, trembling slightly. 'Back when we got in the car with Suzanna or Sonia or whatever her name was?'

I nodded.

'My dad gave me this PSP when I was twelve. I haven't seen him since. I've scratched one mark on it for every time I've spoken to him since then. Every time he's promised to see me and hasn't.'

I stared at him. Glane was right. I didn't see the things that were under my nose. 'I'm sorry,' I stammered. 'I had no—'

'Don't feel sorry,' Jam snapped. 'I don't care about my dad.'

There was an awkward pause.

‘Look,’ I said. ‘It’s not that I want to go off on my own. But I know you think it’s a crap idea . . .’

‘I never said that.’ Jam sighed. ‘It’s just, why do all this by yourself? The police are going to investigate everything. After what Sonia Holtwood did, they’ll have to take the whole idea of you being a missing child seriously. Don’t you see? It’s all going to come out now, whatever anybody does?’

He was right. And that was exactly the problem.

I looked along to the highway. It was cold. And I knew it was risky to even think about hitch-hiking all the way to Evanport. But I couldn’t bear the thought of other people finding my real mum. Other people telling my real family about me. All the officials getting in the way.

I shrugged. ‘I just have to do it, Jam.’

‘OK.’ To my surprise a slow grin spread across his face. ‘Then come back inside for a minute,’ he said. ‘I’ve sorted a much better way for us to get there than hitch-hiking.’

20

Evanport

I lived through so many emotions in the next twenty-four hours, that it's hard to remember how grateful and relieved I was when Jam took me back into the dining room, explaining what he'd arranged. 'I got Glane to agree that if I couldn't talk you out of going, he'd take us to Evanport himself.'

Glane was still at the table. He looked up at me solemnly. 'I cannot let you hitch your ride, Lauren. But I will only help you on condition you tell your parents what you're doing and we call the police as soon as you find this birth family of yours.'

I flung my arms round him. How could I ever have thought Glane was a weirdo? 'Thank you,' I breathed. 'Thank you for everything.'

'Oh well,' Glane said gruffly. 'Evanport is not so far out of my way to Boston.'

We set off as soon as we'd finished eating. I was anxious to get going now, full of butterflies in my stomach about Mum and Dad arriving and somehow stopping us.

We called them from Glane's hired truck. There was more shouting and tears from Mum. They were just about to leave Boston to come and find us.

I told her she and Dad and Carla should stay put until we called the next day, then hung up and switched off the phone. I didn't even bother to try and explain what I was doing.

Mum and Dad didn't deserve an explanation.

We stopped at a motel for a few hours sleep. Well, the others slept – I could hear Glane snoring through the thin walls. I lay awake. The idea that I might actually meet my real mother tomorrow was both exciting and terrifying.

I closed my eyes and tried to remember her face. Her voice. Her gentle smile.

Everything will be all right when I see her.

We arrived at Evanport the next morning, Wednesday, at about 10 am. The main street in the town was crowded with cars and shoppers.

She could be here. She could be one of these people . . .

My heart thumped against my chest.

We passed little clothes shops with wooden porches, and diners with knots of high stools in the windows. The town had a big marina at one end, and lots of the stores in the nearby streets seemed to have something to do with sailing and boats. Many of them had old-fashioned tin signs hung outside: *Yachters' Paradise. Sails at Sea. Tom's Chandlery.*

As the truck rolled slowly down the street I noticed how slim and smart most of the people strolling about were. There were a few younger people, but most of them were middle-aged women with styled hair and neatly pressed tops, and men in chinos with jumpers knotted over their shoulders.

I was so nervous now I thought I was going to be sick. My breath was coming in short, sharp gasps.

I checked myself in the rearview mirror. God I looked terrible. Drawn, ash-white face with rough, raw, red patches on the cheeks.

I wanted to tell Glane to stop so that I could buy some make-up. But I would have had to ask him for the money and, anyway, the more scared I got, the less able I felt to say anything at all.

I felt my confidence sink even further as I looked down at the combats and sweatshirt I was wearing.

'Hey. You OK, Lazerbrain?' Jam nudged me with his arm. I leaned against him, trying to make myself breathe properly.

'I wish I looked better,' I croaked. I wanted it to come out all light and jokey. Instead it sounded as desperate as I felt.

Jam half-turned to me, so he could whisper in my ear. 'I think you look beautiful.'

I blushed.

'When this is over,' he whispered, 'there's something I want to ask you.'

With a crunch of the gears, Glane stopped the truck. As he switched off the engine there was this deafening silence. Blood pounded in my ears.

'We are here,' Glane said.

I sat glued to my seat as Glane opened the door and got out. He stepped back. Somehow I made my legs move as I followed him onto the pavement, my eyes on the house opposite.

It was big – far bigger than our house at home, with a large, neatly mown front lawn. The trees on either side of the grass were golden-leafed, almost glittering in the bright, hard sunshine.

I stood, my hands shaking, staring at the brick path that led up to the front door.

Jam got out of the truck. He came and stood beside me.

'Lauren?'

'I can't do this,' I whimpered. I took a step back to the truck. 'I can't.'

'You want to leave?' Glane said. 'Shall we call your parents? The police?'

'No.' I couldn't back out now. This was what I wanted, wasn't it? The chance to find out for myself whether I was Martha Lauren Purditt. To meet my real mother. In my own way.

I was probably wrong anyway. I would get there and it would be obvious the missing girl wasn't me.

Oh God.

My whole body trembled.

Jam put his hand on my arm. 'Do you want us to come with you?' he said.

I shook my head. I didn't trust myself to speak. But I knew that I had to do this alone. I took a step towards the brick path.

I felt Jam's fingers twist through mine and slide away. 'Good luck, Lazerbrain,' he whispered.

I smiled at him, then turned and walked towards the house.

PART TWO
FINDING LAUREN

21

Inside

A girl opened the door. She was about my height, but maybe a bit younger than me, with long, dyed blonde hair that hung dead straight past her shoulders. I searched her face, desperate for any sign of family resemblance.

She looked at me suspiciously. 'Can I help you?'

'I . . . I . . .' Now I was here, I realised I had absolutely no idea what to say. My legs felt like jelly.

The girl's eyes narrowed. 'What do you want?' she said.

For a second I thought I was going to throw up. It took all my strength just to speak: 'I'm looking for Mrs Purditt,' I said. 'Martha's mother.'

The girl frowned.

'It's Martha I've come about,' I said, wondering for one horrible moment whether I'd even got the right house. 'She went missing a . . . a long time ago.'

For a second the girl looked shocked. Then the surprise in her eyes morphed into contempt.

'Who put you up to this?' she said. 'Was it Amy Brighthouse?'

I blinked, utterly bewildered.

'Who is it, Shelby?' a woman's voice called from the house.

'Go away,' hissed the girl. 'What you're doing is sick. It's so totally uncool I can't believe it.'

She pushed me backwards along the path, then stepped outside the house, pulling the door to behind her. I stared at her. What was she talking about? The girl shoved me in the chest. Hard. I stumbled backwards again.

Behind her, the front door opened. A middle-aged woman with short, flicky black hair appeared in the doorway.

It took me a few seconds to register who she must be.

The woman smiled at me, but her eyes were dull and sad.

I stared at her face. *It can't be you. It can't be.*

'Hello?' she said. 'Are you one of Shelby's friends?'

'No, Mom. She's here on some sicko dare.'

I barely heard them. Tears filled my eyes. The woman in front of me might have been beautiful once, but now there were deep lines carved across her forehead and her skin was sallow and saggy.

This couldn't be my mother.

My mother didn't have pain etched across her face.

The woman looked puzzled. 'Who are you?'

She doesn't know me. She doesn't recognise me.

Both of them were frowning at me now. The air crackled with tension.

There was nothing left but to say it. My voice sounded flat and distant, as if someone else was speaking.

'I think I might be Martha.'

The words hung in the silence between us.

The woman's eyes widened. Her mouth fell open. 'Martha?' she whispered. 'My Martha?'

'You total freak show.' Shelby pushed me again. But I didn't take my eyes off the woman. She stood back, opening the door wide behind her.

'Come in,' she said.

'No,' Shelby shrieked. 'No way. Don't you see? She's doing it for a dare.'

Ignoring her, I followed the woman inside. I got a vague impression of an open space with polished wood cabinets and big, flowery sofas off to the left.

I was numb. It didn't feel real.

'It's not her, Mom,' Shelby shouted, marching up to the woman and shaking her arm. 'Mom? Oh for God's sake! I'm going to get Dad.' She ran out of the house.

The woman led me towards one of the sofas.

'Sit down.'

I sat. The woman perched on the sofa opposite. It felt like her eyes were drinking me up.

I looked away, confused. It shouldn't be like this. If this

was my real mother, surely I would sense it somehow; feel some . . . some connection to her?

The woman bit her lip. 'Do you remember me?'

'I don't know,' I said. I looked down at my lap.

A long silence stretched out between us. In the end I glanced up. The woman was still staring at me.

'What makes you think you're Martha?'

I told her everything that had happened from the day I found the missing poster of Martha on the internet.

As I explained how Sonia had abandoned us in the woods she came and sat next to me. 'Poor baby,' she said.

She lifted her hand, as if she was going to stroke my hair off my face. I drew away, embarrassed.

A dull weight seemed to settle in my chest. This wasn't what I'd expected. I'd thought if I saw her I would know. For sure.

But I didn't. She was just a woman.

Angry voices sounded by the front door. I stood up.

Shelby ran into the room. A little girl – a bit younger than Rory, I guessed – was beside her. Then three middle-aged men strode in – they were all wearing chinos and check shirts, just like the people I'd seen in the Evanport shops. There were too many faces to take in. I looked from one to the other, bewildered.

'Is that her?' The tallest of the men stepped over to me. He gripped my shoulder. There was something almost desperate in his eyes. 'Who are you?' He shook my arm. 'What are you doing here?'

The woman put her hand over his. 'It's Martha, Sam,' she breathed. 'I really think it is.'

At her words pandemonium broke out. Everyone in the room started talking at once. The man began shouting at the woman, completely ignoring me.

'This isn't her, Annie. She's not just going to walk in—'

'It is. She has.' Annie burst into tears. 'Don't you see, sh—'

'Stop it.' The man's voice rose to a terrible roar. 'Stop it. Stop it. I can't take you doing this any more.'

Annie clutched at the man's arm. 'Listen to me,' she sobbed. 'Calm down, Sam, please.'

I glanced round the room. Shelby and the other men were all talking at the tops of their voices by the door. The only person who wasn't speaking was the little girl. She stared at me, open-mouthed from behind the sofa.

My heart was hammering like mad. Whatever I'd imagined finding my real family would be like, it wasn't like this. I didn't want to be here any more. But my legs felt rooted to the spot.

The argument between the man and Annie grew more hysterical.

She was almost on her knees, pleading with him: 'Look at her, look at her, she looks just like you.'

The man didn't seem to hear her: 'I can't take this, Annie,' he kept saying, his face twisted in agony. 'You have to let go.'

'Please stop shouting,' I said. But the words were drowned in the noise around me.

And then a deep voice boomed over all the others. 'QUIET.'

Everyone spun round. Glane was standing in the doorway, his huge presence dominating the room.

Shocked silence.

Before anyone had a chance to ask him who he was or what he was doing there, Glane smiled.

'I think perhaps everyone should be calm and listen to Lauren.'

22
Confession

I was at Evanport police station.

Glane had gone. Jam had gone. All the Purditts had gone.

I'd been talking to an FBI agent for the last two hours.

MJ Johnson was tall with a long, horsey face. I liked her. She'd listened carefully to everything I'd told her and asked lots of questions in a sympathetic drawl.

She'd gone away for a bit, then come back to tell me that Taylor Tarsen had been taken in for questioning and that my description of Sonia Holtwood was being circulated to local law enforcement across the north-east of America.

I knew this was good news. But my mind was still on my meeting with the Purditts. I kept trying to match the sad-eyed Annie Purditt I'd met today, with the angel-faced woman in my dream memory. Were they really the same person?

'Lauren?'

I looked up. MJ stretched out her long legs. 'You need

to understand,' she said. 'There's two separate issues here. This whole business of you maybe being stolen from your birth family when you were little. That's one. But then there's also what Tarsen and Sonia Holtwood planned to do to you and your friend. Those are two separate crimes. Two different, but overlapping investigations.'

'So what's going to happen next?'

'You mean to you?' MJ stood up.

I nodded.

'Your parents'll be here real soon,' she said vaguely. We'll take it from there.'

She left me on my own again. I curled up in my chair and laid my head on my arm.

The seconds on the clock in the room ticked by.

I hadn't told MJ that I was sure Mum and Dad knew about me being kidnapped as a little girl. I could barely think about it myself. I certainly wasn't ready to see them.

I needed time to think about what had happened with the Purditts. I must have been wrong about them. I must have. Surely, if Annie was really my mother, I would have felt something more when I saw her.

I closed my eyes. Tears prickled at the lids. The only person I wanted to see right now was Jam. If my questioning was over for now, maybe his would be soon.

The door opened. I jerked upright, hoping it would be him.

Mum and Dad stood in the doorway.

My mouth fell open. Dad looked as if he'd aged ten years. As for Mum – her face was grey and she seemed bonier than ever. Her jumper hung limply from her shoulders.

For a second they just looked at me. And then, somehow, Mum had crossed the room and was beside me, half shaking me, half pulling me into this hug.

I stood there – stiff and awkward.

Mum's tears splashed onto my neck.

'Oh, Lauren, you stupid, stupid . . . Thank God you're all right.'

She drew back slightly, her hands still on my shoulders. Her eyes sought out mine – fearful, questioning.

Dad moved closer but still stood, his arms folded, staring at me. He looked furious.

Everything had changed. I knew it in that instant. Nothing could ever be the same between us, again.

'Do you have any idea what you've done?' Mum whispered.

I stared at her. What *I'd* done?

'I had to know the truth,' I said.

Dad gave this low growl. I looked at him again. There were dark rings under his eyes and his cheeks were flat and pale.

Mum pulled me down onto one of the chairs. 'We didn't

tell you because we didn't want you to be hurt,' she said. 'We would have told you more when you were ready.'

She still didn't get it. She still didn't realise I knew.

'And just when did you think I would be ready to hear that you'd stolen me away from my real family?'

Mum looked as if I'd slapped her. 'What?'

I stared at her, disgusted. 'Don't lie to me, I know about Sonia Holtwood, remem—'

'We didn't take you from another family.' Mum's voice cracked like a whip. 'We adopted you properly, officially.'

Hate boiled up in my heart. I loathed her. I loathed them both.

'I know about Sonia stealing me,' I screamed. 'I know you did too.'

Mum's forehead was creased with frowns. 'No, Lauren, you've got it wrong.'

I jammed my hands over my ears. I couldn't bear to listen to any more of her lies. Mum pulled at my arms.

'MJ told us what you said, but you have to believe us, we thought you were Sonia's child.'

'So why did you pay her loads of money for me?' I yelled.

Mum blinked at me, her face now chalk-white.

'Come on,' I shrieked. 'You said we'd talk later. Well it *is* later. And we *are* talking. So tell me.'

Mum covered her face with her hands. Dad sat down

opposite us. He still hadn't touched me. Still hadn't said a word.

'Well, Dad?' Tears were spilling down my cheeks. 'You gonna lie to me too?'

He leaned forward and took Mum's hands away from her face.

'Lauren needs to know the whole story.'

Mum gasped. 'But . . .'

Dad shushed her with a squeeze of his hand. He turned to me, his jaw clenched.

'I think it's time you saw this situation from somebody else's point of view, Lauren.'

I glared at him.

'We've often told you how much we wanted you. How special you were to us.' Dad took a deep breath. 'But there are lots of things you don't know.'

He sounded like a different person. His red-cheeked, bumbling self was gone. In its place was this stranger – icy and calm.

'We spent ten years trying to have a baby, Lauren. Eight full IVF cycles and countless other failed attempts. We tried everything. You will never have any idea of what we went through. What your mother went through.' He paused. 'In the end she had a breakdown.'

'Dave, no,' Mum whispered.

'Lauren's asked for this.' Dad looked up at me, a

horrible, cold look in his eyes. 'Your mother tried to commit suicide.'

It was like he'd whacked me in the stomach. I caught my breath. Mum was so organised. So in control of . . . of everything. How could she ever have tried to kill herself?

'Dave,' Mum pleaded.

'So, we agreed, no more IVF. But after a while your mother seemed stronger and, as we both still wanted a child, we decided to try adoption. Of course, with a history of mental illness it was impossible to get local adoption agencies to even consider us. So we started looking further afield. We called agencies all over the world. Tried everywhere from China to Canada. Your mother got more and more depressed and I got more and more scared that . . . that she might . . .'

Dad gazed deep into my eyes.

I looked away.

'Anyway,' he went on, 'one day we got a call from Marchfield. Taylor Tarsen. He'd heard on the grapevine we'd been looking everywhere for a child. He was sympathetic. But he said we would have to bend a few rules to get what we wanted.'

My heart thumped.

'Tarsen told us there was a young woman, Sonia Holtwood, with a little girl. The adoption would be straightforward. But there was a catch. The woman wanted more than the normal expenses that get paid by adoptive parents to birth parents. In short, she wanted to sell you. For a lot of money.'

At last. He'd admitted it. Rage surged through me.

'So you bought me,' I spat. 'Like a car. Like a "thing".' My hands were clenched so tightly the nails were digging into my palms. 'How did it work? Wads of cash in a brown envelope, or something?'

Dad blinked at me.

'Oh no, of course,' I said, sarcastically. 'I forgot. You're an accountant. That must have made it easier.'

'Please, Lauren,' Mum sobbed. 'Maybe giving Sonia all that money was wrong . . .' Her face crumpled.

'You think?'

Dad's fist smashed down onto the chair arm beside him. 'How dare you speak to us like this,' he shouted, 'as if you can sit in judgement on us. You have no sodding idea of what we went through. How we agonised over what we were doing. We paid that money because we wanted a child so badly. We would never have done it if Sonia had been a good mother. If she'd wanted you. If she'd shown the slightest bit of interest in anything except how much cash she could screw out of us.' He stopped, his breath heavy and uneven. 'We're not the villains here.'

'We thought we were rescuing you from her.' Mum took my hand. 'And you rescued us too. Having you made me strong again. Strong enough to try IVF one last time. That's why I always say Rory is such a miracle. But you were my first miracle. You'll always be our daughter, Lauren. Always.'

Mum's whole face was contorted, pleading with me to understand. I closed my eyes, letting what they had just said sink in. They hadn't known I was a stolen child. That was what they were telling me. They'd only paid Sonia money for me because they wanted to save me and because . . . because . . . I opened my eyes and stared at Mum. I was suddenly aware of how little she was. How fragile. Somewhere, underneath the anger, I felt a fluttering of pity for her, for both of them.

'I've worked long hours in a job I hate for eleven years to pay back the money we borrowed,' Dad said, bitterly.

My anger rose again, swamping the pity. 'I didn't ask you to do that.'

Dad sighed. 'No. You didn't, but—'

'You have to understand, we're frightened, Lauren.' Mum squeezed my hand. 'We broke the law. We didn't think we were hurting anyone else. But we still broke the law.'

A sharp rap on the door. MJ walked in. 'Sorry to interrupt,' she said. 'But there're some practical issues we need to discuss.'

I drew my hand out of Mum's and sat up. Mum tensed beside me.

MJ stood in the corner of the room, her hands behind her back. 'So far we have no evidence that Sonia Holtwood isn't your biological mother, Lauren. But if she did kidnap you when you were three, that sure gives her a motive for trying to organise your permanent disappearance now. We've got your file from the Marchfield Adoption Agency – the one you say wasn't there when you broke in. We're checking out all the details. But that's going to take a bit of time. And the Purditts are, naturally, all stirred up to know one way or the other.'

I glanced at Mum's hand on the seat beside me. She was gripping it so hard her knuckles were white.

MJ cleared her throat. 'There is something that can speed things up and tell us whether or not you're their daughter in just a few hours.' She paused. 'A DNA test.'

23 Night fears

The DNA test took less than a minute. The same nurse who'd checked me over when we arrived at the police station put a swab – like a cotton bud – in my mouth and swiped it against the inside of my cheek. She said the results would be ready first thing tomorrow.

I couldn't believe so much rested on something so quick and easy to do.

The FBI let Mum and Dad take me back to the Evanport Hotel. I knew Jam and his mum were here too. I kept asking to see Jam, but Mum made me stay in her and Dad's hotel room. After a while, Rory and Aunt Bea turned up. Aunt Bea's my dad's sister. She'd flown out to help look after Rory when I went missing. I used to get on with her quite well. But right now she kept looking at me as if I'd just crawled out from under a rock.

The tension in the room was terrible. Mum was pretending that we hadn't had our conversation. That I didn't know she'd tried to top herself years back. She marched around, folding clothes that were already folded, wiping surfaces that had already been cleaned by the chambermaid, and talking about nothing.

Rory was whiny and aggressive. Not surprising, I suppose. He had, after all, missed his entire trip to the *Legends of the Lost Empire* ride at Fantasma. I tried to say sorry to him for messing up his holiday, but he stuck his fingers in his ears and pretended he couldn't hear me.

Dad just mooched moodily round the room, hunched over like a bear.

All I wanted was to see Jam.

At last Aunt Bea and Dad took Rory off for an ice cream, leaving Mum and me on our own. A few minutes later Mum went to the bathroom. As soon as she'd shut the door, I picked up the phone by the bed and asked reception to put me through to Jam Caldwell.

'Password please?' the receptionist drawled.

'Password?' I frowned.

The receptionist made a clicking sound with her tongue. 'Yes ma'am. I'm sorry but I'm not authorised to connect you or tell you the room number without you giving me the password.'

I stared at the phone, but before I could say anything else, Mum's hand reached over my shoulder and pressed down on the dialtone button.

I spun round. 'What's going on, Mum?'

'We don't want you seeing him.'

'What . . . ?' I stared at her, completely bewildered. 'Why? He's my best friend. None of this is his fault.'

'He encouraged you to run away from us.'

This was so unfair, I lost my temper on the spot.

'He came with me to help me. He actually tried to talk me out of going to find Sonia Holtwood.'

'It's not just that,' Mum said. The bony ridges of her cheekbones flushed pink. 'You were on your own with him for several nights. We need to talk about . . . about the implications of that.'

'What?' She couldn't be serious.

But she was.

It came down to this – I might have travelled across three states, been kidnapped and left for dead in an icy wood, and discovered I'd been stolen and sold as a three-year-old, but all Mum was interested in was what I'd got up to with Jam.

It was so ridiculous that I laughed. 'For the seven millionth time, he's not my boyfriend.'

Mum pursed her lips. It was clear she didn't believe me.

'But, Mum, he's my friend.' Fear snaked down my spine as what she was saying sank in. I couldn't survive without Jam. No way. My voice rose in panic. 'You can't stop me from seeing him.'

'We can and we will,' Mum snapped.

And that – as far as she was concerned – was that.

After Rory and I had been moved into our own room, I spent the rest of the day wandering miserably around the hotel. I hoped I'd bump into Jam or Carla, but I didn't. When it got dark I came up and sat looking out of the window at the lights twinkling along the marina.

Mum ordered food for me and Rory to eat in the room, then she and Dad went downstairs to the hotel restaurant. They didn't even ask if I wanted to go with them.

Mum just said: 'Tomorrow's a big day. Dad and I need to talk.'

I picked at my food, trying to ignore the endless cartoons playing on the TV in our room. Too many thoughts were crowding in on me – all the stuff about Mum and Dad being desperate for a baby, whether Sonia Holtwood had been caught yet, and, of course, what it would mean if I really was Martha Lauren Purditt.

I'd only ever thought about it as a kind of fantasy before. An alternative life which I could make up to suit my mood. Now I'd met the Purditts I was painfully aware that there was a whole family reality behind my fantasy. A family reality I was not at all sure I wanted to face.

I tried to distract myself by playing I Spy with Rory, but he lost interest after one round and went back to his cartoons.

Mum came in at about ten o'clock, threw a wobbly that Rory still had the telly on, wiped tomato ketchup off his face and left again.

I pretended to be asleep.

As the night wore on, my thoughts became darker, more insistent. When I turned away from one, another pushed its way into my head. I found myself imagining how Mum had tried to kill herself. Then it was Sonia Holtwood – I saw her in my mind's eye waiting and watching outside the hotel room door. In the end I had to get up and go out into the corridor to prove to myself she wasn't there.

Get a grip, Lauren.

As I lay down again in bed I caught sight of my suitcase, standing forlornly in the corner. Mum had brought it with her from Boston Airport. Waves of guilt washed over me as I remembered how haggard she and Dad had looked when they'd seen me earlier.

I shuddered. Suppose Mum'd got so distraught not knowing what'd happened to me that she'd tried to kill herself again?

I turned over and plumped up my pillow. Where was Jam? I missed him so badly. He was the only person I knew who let me be completely myself. Though what had he said? That I was the most self-obssessed person he'd ever met?

Maybe I was. Maybe it was true.

I slept for a while, then woke up as it was getting light. I lay on my back, listening to Rory snuffling like a piglet in the next bed.

I tried not to think about what being the Purditt's daughter would mean. They would want to see me again, which was fine – I was curious about them, too. But it wasn't going to be easy.

Suppose they wanted to call me Martha?

Suppose they expected me to call them Mum and Dad?

There was a gentle rap at the door. I sat up and looked across the room. Another rap, slightly louder this time.

I scrambled out of bed and padded across the thick, hotel carpet. Rory was still breathing deep, snorty breaths. I stood at the door and listened. My heart raced. Had I imagined it?

'Lauren,' whispered a low voice. 'It's me.'

24

DNA

Jam.

I pulled open the door. He was dressed. Green T-shirt and jeans. His eyes looked almost gold in the dim light of the hotel corridor. I felt this weird jolt in my stomach. His face was so cute. Why hadn't I noticed before? The slope of his nose. The little knot in his eyebrow. The smooth curve of his lips.

'They won't let me see you,' Jam looked furtively up and down the corridor. 'I had to give the receptionist this big sob-story just to get your room number.'

'Oh,' I said. I could feel my face reddening. This was Jam, for goodness' sake. My best friend. But suddenly I had no idea what to say to him.

Jam didn't seem to notice how awkward I was being. He was frowning down at the floor, as if he was trying to make up his mind about something. 'Lauren,' he said. His voice was low, husky. It sent a shiver down my spine. 'D'you remember me saying there was something I wanted to ask you?'

I stepped closer to him. So close I could see each individual eyelash around his eyes. My heart was beating fast. He looked up. And then I saw it. I saw what he wanted to ask me. I saw what everyone else had been seeing for months.

'Yes?' My breath caught in my throat.

Jam was looking at me, moving nearer. Nearer.

I closed my eyes as his lips pressed – warm and soft – against my mouth. I felt this fizzing in the pit of my stomach and – and yes, I know it's a major cliché – my knees went all weak, like they wouldn't hold me up.

I drew back and opened my eyes.

Jam smiled at me.

My insides melted like lipstick on a radiator.

'Ugh. Are you *kissing*?' I jumped. Rory was standing less than a metre away from us, inside the room, his snubby nose wrinkled in distaste.

Voices echoed in the distance. Then footsteps. Louder and louder, stampeding towards us.

In seconds the corridor was full of people. Jam was still smiling, gorgeously, at me. As if he hadn't even noticed anyone else was here.

'Good, Lauren you're awake.' MJ Johnson strode over, forcing me to tear my eyes away from Jam.

'Get inside the room, please.'

Her voice was strained. Urgent. I looked round at the

other agents, behind her. They were carrying guns in their hands.

'What is it?' I said.

MJ ignored me. She tried to spin Jam away from the door. 'Back to your room, buddy.'

For a split-second I thought maybe she'd seen us kissing. But immediately I knew that would hardly explain the other agents and the guns.

'What's happening?' I said.

Jam was still standing in the corridor.

'Move,' MJ barked at him.

'I'm staying with Lauren.'

The other agents were hammering on Mum and Dad's door.

'Oh, for goodness' sake, all right then. Inside. Now,' MJ ordered. She pushed the three of us into the hotel room, then shut the door. I glanced at the clock by the bed: 6.30 am. Why were they waking Mum and Dad up this early?

'Hey, Rory,' MJ said. 'Wanna watch TV next door?'

Rory nodded eagerly. Mum was always dead strict about TV in the morning. MJ spoke quietly to one of the other agents, who took Rory out of the room. Then MJ walked over to where I was perched on the side of the bed.

She held up a piece of paper. 'Your DNA results,' she said.

I knew before she told me.

'According to the test there's a greater than 99.9% chance that you are the biological offspring of Annie and Sam Purditt.'

In other words, no doubt at all.

After all this time and effort to find out where I came from, I thought I would feel excited. Or afraid. Or at least relieved.

But I felt nothing.

Jam sat beside me on the bed. He took my hand from my lap and twisted his fingers through mine.

There was a sharp rap at the door. One of the male FBI agents poked his head round and nodded at MJ. 'Targets secure,' he said.

'What targets?' I said.

MJ sighed. 'This is real hard for you Lauren, I know, but the fact that you are confirmed as Martha Lauren Purditt means that we now know you were abducted from here in Evanport that September, then adopted two-and-a-half months later, under an alias, from the Marchfield Adoption Agency in Marchfield, Vermont. What we don't know is how many people were involved in the abduction and the cover-up and fraud that followed.' She paused. 'It's possible that your adoptive parents knew what was going on.'

'No.' My mouth was dry. 'They didn't know. They thought Sonia Holtwood was my mother.'

'I'm sorry, Lauren,' MJ said. 'But your adoptive parents have been taken in for questioning and until our investigations are complete they will be allowed no further contact with you.'

No. I thought about the agents with the guns.

MJ squatted down in front of me. 'It's just an investigation. There's no evidence against them. But we need to see their paperwork around the adoption. Bank account data. That sort of thing.'

My heart thumped. Bank data? When the FBI knew about the money Mum and Dad had illegally paid Sonia, they'd look as guilty as hell. I looked down. 'How long's the investigation going to take?'

MJ shrugged. 'We're already checking out all the adoption agency files. It's going to take a while to work out who exactly forged all the records and certificates to do with your birth and early years. And then we have to find out who at the agency was supposed to check things like the hospital where you were born – and whether they didn't bother or, more likely, whether they were paid to falsify the information.'

'But none of that has anything to do with Mum and Dad,' I protested.

Jam put his arm round my shoulders.

MJ said nothing.

'Will I have to stay here with Rory and Aunt Bea?'

‘I think your aunt is planning to take Rory back to England in the next couple of days,’ MJ said.

I frowned. ‘But what about me?’ I glanced at Jam. ‘Can I stay here with . . . with Carla?’

MJ shook her head. ‘We’ve agreed Ms Caldwell can take Jam back to England too. We’ve got his statement. And until we find Sonia Holtwood there’s nothing else he can do here.’

I looked up at Jam, my heart pounding.

‘I’ll talk to Mum. See if I can get her to let me stay,’ he said. But there was no conviction in his voice.

I turned back to MJ ‘So what’s going to happen to me?’

‘Well, there will be an *ex-parte* proceeding within twenty-four hours. That will result in temporary orders as to your custody. Then after a month, there’ll be a properly ordered hearing and permanent orders which will decide where you live permanently.’

Permanently.

The word slid round my head.

‘I don’t understand.’

‘I’m sorry, Lauren. It’s complicated.’ MJ paused. ‘Look. Although we know you’re the Purditt’s daughter, your adoption to the UK has to be legally proved to be invalid. In about a month’s time there’ll be a hearing to do just that. At the hearing the judge will overturn the illegal adoption and decide exactly where you should live and who should have custody over you. Permanently. In the meantime the normal procedure for any minor whose parentage is in dispute is for you to be placed with Social Services under a foster care arrangement. Then—'

'Foster care?' I breathed. 'You mean staying with strangers?'

MJ patted my knee. 'They'd be good people, Lauren, properly vetted by the state and—'

'But I don't want to go and stay with people I don't know.'

'Listen. You're not letting me finish. I said, normally the state would find foster carers for you. But this is not a normal situation. The Purditts know about the DNA result. My guess is that they're going to get a family court judge to approve a "best interest placement".'

'What does that mean?' I leaned against Jam. I couldn't believe what was happening.

'The Purditts are most likely going to get themselves approved as temporary foster parents.' MJ smiled. 'They're wealthy people, with good standing in the community. If they can get Social Services to rush through the necessary criminal background and fingerprint checks and stuff, *and* persuade a judge you would be better off with them than anyone else, then you could stay with them until the permanent orders are issued and they can fight your adoptive parents for custody.'

I stared at her, blankly.

Go and live with the Purditts?

'Look at it this way, Lauren,' MJ sighed. 'After eleven years, you'd be going home.'

25

String

The Purditts did exactly what MJ had predicted. Which meant that, twenty-four hours later, I found out I was going to be living with them until the court hearing to resolve permanent custody took place at the end of November.

MJ forced me to see a counsellor the next day. She said I should talk to somebody to help me adjust to the new situation I was in.

To be honest, talking about everything just made me feel worse. The stupid counsellor was ancient. She kept nodding sympathetically at me and saying 'Mmn, very difficult for you,' until I wanted to scream at her.

I know it's difficult. What can I do about it?

I was sure part of her was thinking: *What's your problem? You wanted to know who you were. Well here it is – you're Martha Lauren Purditt. Get on with it.*

It was so hard to explain how I felt. I'd had to go through it with the judge already.

'I'd rather live with the Purditts than foster parents who've got nothing to do with me,' was what I'd said. But in my heart my feelings were all muddled. Of course I wanted to spend time with the Purditts, but I didn't want to live with them. I didn't *know* them. The thought of moving in with them was terrifying.

And I missed Mum and Dad.

I had only one hope – that the counsellor could persuade Carla and the Purditts to let Jam come with me. If he was there, maybe the whole thing would be bearable.

I had lunch with a distracted Aunt Bea and an unusually subdued Rory, then waited anxiously for the counsellor to come back for our second session. As soon as she walked in I knew it was bad news.

'We all hear what you're saying, Lauren. And Mr and Mrs Purditt sympathise.' The counsellor paused, her fleshy face creased in a patronising frown. 'But everyone feels there will be enough for you to adjust to without your boyfriend complicating things.'

'He's not my boyfriend,' I muttered. I couldn't look her in the eye as I said it. I mean, it's still true, I guess. I'm not so naïve that I think one kiss makes you someone's girlfriend.

'The only other option is that Jam's mother may be able to stay on here a little longer. That way at least you'll still be able to keep in touch.'

I'd only seen Carla once since we'd been in the hotel. Jam said she spent most of her time exploring Evanport's antique and craft stores. In the end I caught up with her browsing the jewellery in the hotel gift shop.

'Darling.' Carla smiled as I walked over. She ran a heavily-ringed hand over a display of wooden necklaces, then picked one up. It was painted red and gold and brown, the colour of autumn leaves. 'Look at this. I bet it's Native American.'

I didn't know what to say to that.

'So.' Carla raised her eyes. 'I didn't like to mention it in front of your parents, but our little session helped didn't it?

I blinked, not understanding.

'You know,' she said. 'The hypnotherapy? I knew you'd felt something – even though you said you hadn't. It's what led you here, isn't it?' She leaned closer. 'I wish you'd told me at the time. I could have talked to Mrs Worrybags for you. Avoided us getting into this mess.'

I wondered what on earth she thought she could have said about me tracking down my birth parents that Mum would have listened to.

Carla weighed the necklace in her hand. 'I can almost feel the earth's energy pulsing through the beads. I love America. It's so big, so modern, and yet there's still so much *nature*.'

'Carla?' I cleared my throat. 'Wouldn't you like to stay here longer?'

'Of course, darling, I'd—' Carla stopped in mid-sentence. She put the necklace down and sighed. 'I'd love nothing better. You know that. But I've got the girls to get back to. And my clients. And Jam should really be at school. Apart from anything else, he's not exactly top of his class. Still, that's boys for you. Lazy. Uncommunicative. Only one thing on their minds.'

I blushed. 'Jam's not like that.'

Carla raised an eyebrow as she fingered a brooch in the shape of a star.

'Mum always says boys are easier,' I said.

Carla snorted. 'Darling, I adore Jam, but men are basically creatures from a different planet. I'm pretty sure I was some European king in a former life and you wouldn't believe the . . .'

As Carla droned on about her out-of-body experiences, I leaned my head against the window of the shop. I couldn't imagine a future without Mum and Dad and Jam. I had thought knowing for sure that I was Martha Lauren Purditt would make sense of everything. I thought finding my real mother would fill up all the missing parts of me.

But Martha Lauren was just the name of a missing girl.

And Annie Purditt didn't look like the beautiful woman in my memory.

And I was more alone than ever.

I was packed and ready to leave when MJ arrived to collect me at two-thirty the following afternoon.

I'd said goodbye to Rory that morning with more of a pang than I would have thought possible. I wondered when I would see him again. Auntie Bea wanted to hurry home to start organising Mum and Dad's lawyers and all the bank stuff.

I tried not to think about Mum and Dad too much. Jam was dead practical of course. 'The Feds can't hold them without any evidence. It's not like they're terrorists. They'll be released in a day or two. And once you've explained to the Purditts you don't want to stay with them, they won't force you. They can't.'

I thought about the money Mum and Dad had paid Sonia Holtwood. And the hunger on Annie Purditt's face when she saw me. My heart sank. But I didn't say any more. I didn't want to spoil the last few hours we had together.

Jam had snuck into my room as soon as Aunt Bea and Rory left. At first it was kind of awkward. I wasn't used to being so self-conscious with him – worrying about how I looked or what he really thought about me. But Jam was brilliant. He said he'd really liked me for months. Wasn't it weird that I hadn't even noticed? Anyway, he was sweet and funny and . . . Well. All I can say is my packing took a long time.

And then MJ knocked on the door.

'Time to go.' She looked at our faces. 'You've got two minutes.' She stepped outside and shut the door.

This was it. Jam wasn't flying home until the following evening. But everyone had made it clear I wouldn't see him again before he went.

I would be too busy bonding with my new family.

I stared at him, my heart in my mouth.

'Don't go.'

He smiled his big, cute grin at me.

'I'll come back.'

No you won't. No you won't. Oh my God, you'll forget me as soon as the first girl comes up to you – and that will be in about five minutes from now, because I've been with you enough times when girls made it obvious they liked you and I can't bear it – you have to wait for me please, please, please.

MJ knocked on the door again. 'Come on, guys.'

There was no more time. Jam just pushed something into my hand, squeezed my fingers over it, and left.

MJ picked up my case. 'Ready?' she said.

I nodded, stumbling blindly after her to the hotel elevator. I could feel whatever Jam had given me, small and smooth against my fingers.

I waited until we were out of the lift and MJ was organising the cars out front. Then I opened my hand. There, in my palm, was a small oval of carved wood with a hole through the middle. Like the pieces I had seen in Glane's cabin, only much smaller and simpler.

He made this for me.

I asked the reception desk for a length of string, threaded it through the wooden oval and tied it round my neck. Then I followed MJ out to the car.

As she slammed the doors shut, it felt like she was locking me into a prison.

26

Ribbon

The journey to the Purditts' seemed to flash past in seconds. I sat in the back of the car, my hands clenched tightly together.

When I saw the yellow ribbon round the tree in the Purditt's front garden my heart, already in a mush in my shoes, dribbled out onto the ground. 'There's not going to be a party or anything is there?' I said to MJ.

She shot me a puzzled look. 'That ribbon's been there since you disappeared eleven years ago,' she said. 'Didn't you notice it before?'

I hadn't. As we walked up the path I saw she was right. Close to, the ribbon was faded and stained. 'It's a tradition,' MJ said, 'for when people are a long way from home.'

As she rang on the doorbell my heart thumped in my chest. The house seemed quiet, but I was dreading all the people I might have to meet.

Annie Purditt opened the door almost before MJ had stopped pressing the buzzer. She stood back to let me in.

My legs shook as I walked into the house. I got the same

impression I had before. Lots of space and light and polished wooden furniture. This time I noticed a swimming pool through the back-door window.

I stood awkwardly, wondering where everyone else was.

The man who had spoken to me when I was here before was hanging back by one of the flowery sofas. But I could feel his eyes boring into me. I knew his name was Sam Purditt.

My dad. And yet, so not my dad.

I looked at the floor wishing I was anywhere else.

MJ said goodbye. I was trying too hard not to cry to be able to say anything back. Annie Purditt showed MJ out, then came and held out her hand for my suitcase. I gave it up reluctantly. I still hadn't spoken.

'Come and sit down. We're on our own. We thought it would be easier for you.' She put my suitcase by the stairs and led me over to the sofas. I had this strong sense she was dying to hurl herself at me and give me this major hug and was restraining herself with difficulty.

I sat in the corner of the sofa, as far away from her as possible.

I looked down. The wooden oval on its bit of string dangled over my top. The sight of it brought such a lump to my throat that I had to dig my fingers into my palms to stop myself from howling.

'Lauren?' I looked up. Annie was sitting on the sofa

opposite me. Sam stood behind her, reaching over her shoulder. They were holding hands.

They couldn't have been more different from Mum and Dad. Despite the lines on Annie's face, she was obviously much, much younger than Mum and really groomed. Her hair was all carefully set and her make-up immaculate, right down to the glossy pink lipstick. Sam appeared even younger. He was tall and athletic-looking with dark brown hair that flopped over his forehead.

'The counsellor told us you prefer to be called Lauren,' Annie said.

Course I do, it's my name.

'Which is fine,' Sam added quickly.

'Lauren was my mother's name,' Annie went on. 'That's why it's your middle name. I'm so glad that you remembered it – at least, I assume you must have or else . . .' She looked away. 'My mother wasn't much older than you when I was born. Eighteen. She was called Lauren after the famous actress, Lauren Bacall. It's my middle name too.'

'Annie.' Sam patted his wife on the shoulder.

'Yes, I'm sorry, I'm just . . .' A tear trickled down her cheek.

I looked down at my lap. This woman was my mother. I had to live with her. And she was a complete stranger.

'This is so very hard for all of us, Lauren. But . . . but

D— Sam and I want you to know that we love you so, so much.'

You don't know me.

I suddenly missed Mum and Dad unbearably.

Oh God, what if they get sent to prison and I never see them again?

My gut twisted.

'We never stopped waiting and searching and hoping and praying you would come home to us. Oh . . . oh what is it?'

I couldn't hold the tears back any longer. At the word 'home' my whole body just heaved in despair. I bent over, hiding my face, every part of me racked with silent sobs.

And suddenly they were both there, in floods of tears themselves. Annie at my knees, her arms round me, going, 'My baby, my baby.' Sam's hand stroking my hair.

It was hideous.

I wanted to scream and yell at them to go away. To let me go home. But what good would it do? Mum and Dad weren't allowed to see me. I had no home any more.

I forced myself to stop crying. I sat up, drew back and wiped my eyes.

Mum and Dad are just being questioned. They'll be out soon and then they can fight for me. The Purditts won't make me stay. If they really love me they'll let me go.

I tucked my wooden oval inside my top. I said the words over and over in my head.

Things can only get better.

I didn't know it at the time – but things were about to get a lot worse.

27

r u still missing me?

About an hour after I'd arrived, Annie's and Sam's other daughters turned up.

I remembered them both from the other day – bottle-blonde Shelby, who had tried to make me leave, and little Madison, who had stared at me over the top of the sofa, her eyes as big and round as a bushbaby's.

'Are you sure it's OK?' Shelby said from the front door.

'Of course, sweetie.' Annie stood up. 'Come in and meet your sister properly.'

Shelby shuffled cautiously into the living room. Her hair was tied loosely in a ponytail and she was wearing a massive amount of make-up. I knew from what Annie had told me that she was thirteen, a year younger than me. No way would my mum have let me put that much eyeliner on even now.

'Hi Martha.' She blushed. 'Oh, I'm sorry. I'm supposed to call you Lauren.'

'Hi,' I said, shortly. Then, feeling perhaps I should be a bit more generous, I added: 'I'm sure you'll get used to it.'

Shelby's lip trembled.

'It's OK, sweetikins.' Annie gave her an enormous hug, then turned to me. 'Shelby's just a little emotional right now. She was only two when you went missing, so this is all kind of strange for her.'

Strange for *her*?

Shelby fixed me with her tiny, grey eyes. 'I've always wanted to meet my big sister,' she said, in this flat voice that made it quite clear to me she had never wanted any such thing.

'Oh, Shelbs. What a sweet thing to say.' Annie hugged her again.

I heard a noise behind my chair and looked round. I jumped. Madison was standing by the arm, about half a metre away from me.

'Madi, please don't creep up on people like that,' Annie sighed. 'I'm going to make some tea. Come through when you're ready.'

Shelby followed her mother out of the room. I smiled at Madison. 'Hi.'

She stared at me.

'So how old are you?' I said, though Annie had already told me.

'Six.' Madison still hadn't taken her eyes off me. 'Are you really my sister?'

I nodded.

'I imagined you were a princess.'

'Oh. Well . . . er . . . I'm not. Sorry, I guess I'm just ordinary.'

She leaned forward and whispered in my ear. Her breath smelled of strawberry jam. 'We could still pretend you are.'

I grinned. 'D'you like pretend games?'

Madison nodded solemnly. 'I'm going to be an actress when I grow up.'

'Really? D'you like dressing up and stuff?' I asked, remembering how I used to like putting on Mum's old clothes when I was little.

'Some.' Madison tilted her oval face to one side. 'But what I really like is pretending. You know, imagining being other people.'

'Tea's ready,' Annie called.

Madison skipped out of the room. I followed, watching the way her long dark hair swung from side to side across her back.

'I hope you talked nicely to Lauren,' Annie said as Madison sat down at the table. She turned to me. 'She's such a shy little thing.'

'Such a freak show, you mean,' Shelby said, not particularly under her breath.

Annie appeared not to have heard this.

'Actually Madison was great,' I said loudly. 'She told me . . . lots of stuff.'

Madison reddened. I tried to smile at her, to reassure her I wasn't going to grass her up about her acting ambitions in front of Shelby, but she looked away.

Annie set a jug of milk down on the table. As she reached across my chair I noticed the roll of flesh creeping over the top of her skirt.

Great. Just my luck. On top of everything else.

Fat genes.

At least I got out of the house that afternoon. I'd asked if I could use the phone later.

'Of course.' Annie blushed. 'You don't need to ask.'

'Hey, why don't I take you to the mall?' Sam said. 'You can pick out your own cell.'

So off we went, just Sam, me and Madison, in the big seven-seater family car.

Sam was OK, actually. Really sweet with Madison – gentle and a bit teasing. Not a big talker, though. I guess he's what Carla would call intuitive – he understands stuff without you having to say it.

For instance, we both knew a new phone would take a few hours to charge up. But he could see I was dying to make a call so, without me having to ask, he offered to lend me his mobile. *And* he walked off with Madison round a clothes store while I was on the phone. I mean Mum would have hung around, wanting to know who I was speaking to. And Dad just wouldn't have got the hint. He certainly would never have spent ten minutes looking at shirts and sweaters to give me some privacy.

Who did I call? Jam, of course. He was still at the hotel.

'I miss you,' he said.

It made me feel better. Kind of warm and glowy inside.

Until Carla called him away.

Then I was alone again.

I chose a really neat little silver mobile with a pink trim. Sam said I could have whatever I wanted, so I picked this expensive model with video and camera functions. I wasn't being greedy. It meant Jam would be able to send me pictures and little videos of himself – if he could borrow somebody else's phone to send them on.

Afterwards the three of us drove down to the harbour. It was cold, but in a good way – sharp and crisp with clear blue skies. Evanport is really pretty down by the water. There's a big wooden promenade area with lots of cafés and a long marina full of boats.

We sat and drank a couple of Cokes looking out over the water. Madison drifted about, occasionally shooting me these big-eyed glances. Then Sam showed me his boat. The

Josephine May. It was all sparkly in the sunshine, bobbing about on the water like an impatient kid. Sam got dead excited when we went on board – even had Madison run all over, telling me what the different parts of the boat were called.

'Course I don't get as much time as I'd like to sail,' he said. 'And Annie and Shelby aren't as keen as they used to be. But Madi still loves coming. Maybe we'll take her out sometime.'

He looked at me expectantly.

'Sure,' I said.

The sun was almost set by the time we drove the short journey home. Sam held Madison's hand as they walked indoors. That and the darkness made everything worse. I was so miserable, I didn't even notice MJ's car parked outside.

As soon as we got indoors, I could see from her face it wasn't good news. She took me through to the living area while Annie pottered about in the kitchen, casting anxious glances in our direction.

'Taylor Tarsen's admitted knowing about the whole kidnapping from when you were little,' MJ said.

I frowned. 'But that's good,' I said, 'isn't it? I mean if he's admitted taking me, then that proves Mum and Dad are innocent.'

'It's not that simple,' MJ said. 'Tarsen's signed a

statement saying your parents were involved in the whole thing.'

I stared at her, my heart beating wildly. 'He's lying,' I cried. 'Mum and Dad told me everything. They thought Sonia Holtwood was my mother.'

'Sssh.' MJ leaned closer and patted my arm. 'Between you and me I believe you. Your parents seem like decent folk and their story makes sense. But they've admitted now they broke the law with the money transfer to Sonia. And we have to go through due process.'

We talked a bit more. MJ promised she would get Mum and Dad's lawyer to call me later. Then she slipped away.

I sat on the sofa. Sam's mobile was on the little table by the door. I picked it up and texted Jam. I didn't dare call and speak to him in case anyone in the house came in.

Anyway, what I really wanted was a hug.

Remembering what he'd said earlier I wrote: *r u stl mssng me?*

He texted straight back: *more*.

I deleted both messages and put the phone back. Strange how something can keep you going and break your heart at the same time.

28

Martha's room

I spoke to Mum and Dad's attorney later that evening.

I could hardly take in what he was saying. Mum and Dad had been charged with something awful-sounding, like conspiracy to abduct a minor. They were in prison, waiting for the next stage in what ever the legal process was.

Mr Sanchez, the lawyer, said he was working hard on their behalf but that I needed to prepare myself for a long fight.

I came off the phone too dazed to even speak.

'What is it, Lauren?' Annie hovered round me, all nervy and anxious.

I couldn't bring myself to tell her. 'Nothing,' I said.

'OK . . . well . . . er . . . I've cooked a special dinner,' Annie said. 'It'll be ready in a few minutes.' She fluttered miserably away.

She wasn't joking when she said 'special'. The table was covered with a crisp linen tablecloth with proper napkins and gleaming white china at every place.

I sat down between Sam and Madison, hoping they didn't eat this formally every night.

Annie served out something she called Osso Bucco. We ate in silence. I could feel everyone watching me. I kept my eyes glued to my plate.

'Fork, Madison,' Annie said gently.

I glanced sideways. Madison put down her knife and transferred her fork to the other hand.

I had no idea what was going on, but I felt way too awkward to ask any questions. A few minutes later it happened again.

'Come on, Madison,' Annie said. 'We're eating cuisine.'

Madison blushed and snatched a quick look at me.

Shelby sniggered. 'Just because Mar— er, Lauren, does it, doesn't mean you can.'

I stared at her. Just because I did what?

Annie started flapping. 'It's a small thing, Lauren. We only eat with the fork. I mean, we use the knife and fork together to cut food but then we transfer the fork to the other hand to eat.'

I think my mouth must have dropped open.

Who were these people?

Shelby sniggered again. 'It's because we think it's bad manners to shovel food into our mouths,' she said pointedly, staring at my own fork which was pressed against my knife, gathering a last mouthful of chopped string beans.

'Oh, but we don't expect *you* to do it,' Annie twittered

at me. 'It's just an American thing and everyone knows you've had different . . . I mean you're European. I mean . . .' She shot up from the table and started gathering plates. Still talking her head off, she raced into the kitchen and re-emerged in seconds with a large cake. Holding it high in the air, she advanced to the table.

'I made this while you were out earlier. I wasn't sure but I felt you would understand. This is such a momentous day . . .' Her voice tailed off as she placed the cake in front of me. It was high and covered with white icing. Across the top, in curly yellow letters were the words: *welcome home Lauren*.

'Neat frosting, Mom,' Madison said.

I stared at the cake.

Annie kept on wittering away behind me. She edged a long knife – handle first – towards me across the table. I could feel everyone else's gaze: Sam all concerned, Shelby looking smug, and Madison with those big velvety eyes round like saucers.

I didn't pick up the knife, so Annie reached across and snatched it up herself. Her hand was shaking as she hacked unevenly at the cake.

'Well, I guess you'll want to look round upstairs, Lauren.' She slid a slab of cake onto a small plate and placed it in front of me. 'And we ought to discuss which room you're going to sleep in too.'

I pushed the plate away from me.

No way was I going to eat her stupid cake.

A look of humiliation flickered across Annie's eyes. Her face flushed a deep red. 'What we thought was you could choose. If you'd like you could sleep in with Shelby. We thought that might be fun, so you girls could get to know each other.'

I glanced at Shelby. She glowered at me.

I'd rather get to know a poisonous snake.

'Or you could choose one of the guest rooms and we'll make it over for you while you get used to being here.'

I'll never get used to being here.

'Or . . .' Annie hesitated. 'Or there's your old room.'

I looked up at her. It hadn't occurred to me that I would already have a room in the house. In spite of the homesick ache inside me, I was instantly curious.

'Would you like to see it?' Annie asked.

I nodded.

'OK.' Annie jumped up eagerly, knocking over her glass. Water flooded onto the floor. 'Oh darn, what a mess.'

Sam followed her into the kitchen to get a cloth.

'Why doesn't Shelby show Lauren *her* room first, while we clear up?' he said. 'You can join them in a minute.'

'Sure, Dad.' Shelby turned to me. 'I'd love to,' she whispered sarcastically.

I followed Shelby up the stairs. From behind I could see that although she was the same height as me, her legs were really much shorter. They stuck out from her mini-skirt like tough little tree trunks. I could also see dark-brown roots spreading through the blonde highlights down the back of her head. This made me feel slightly better. A horrible sister was bad enough. But a glamorous, horrible sister with perfect hair and legs up to her eyebrows would have been unbearable.

Shelby stomped across the long corridor. She pointed to an open door on the left. 'That's mine,' she said.

Through the doorway I could see a huge dressing table covered with make-up and perfume bottles. Frilly lilac curtains at the window and a stash of dolls in one corner gave it a little girly feel, but the rest of the room was more grown-up. Clothes were spilling out of a walk-in wardrobe at the end of the bed.

Shelby pulled the door shut in my face. 'You not allowed in there. Especially not my closet,' she said. 'I don't want you touching any of my stuff.'

Did you take lessons in being this mean or were you born naturally gifted?

'Don't worry,' I said, coldly. 'I wouldn't touch your stuff if you paid me.'

Shelby's eyes were like tiny stones. 'Dohn't wahree,' she said, mimicking my accent. She flicked her long hair off her shoulder and stared at the wooden oval on the string round my neck. 'At least I *have* nice stuff.'

I felt the heat rise through my throat.

'No one wants you here, you know,' Shelby sneered. 'Mom and Dad are making out like this is the most awesome thing that's ever happened to them, but what they really want is the you they remember. A toddler. Not a teenager. Look.' She pointed to a door a little further down the corridor.

The name 'Martha' was written on the outside in big letters, each one decorated with a different animal. I stared at the 'M'. It had a monkey painted on the front. I felt the stirring of a memory. This was the first thing in the whole house that felt familiar. I walked right up to the shut door, my stomach churning.

'Well, why don't you go in?' Shelby said. 'It's your room.'

I turned the handle. It was a huge room – all bright, primary colours. The walls were yellow, with an alphabet frieze up by the ceiling.

A wooden trunk stood under the window, covered with a pile of dolls and teddy bears.

I wandered over to the single bed beyond the trunk. A blue rabbit with big button eyes lay on top of the soft coverlet. I picked it up. The rabbit was wearing a pink satin ballgown with thin straps. It was worn and one of the long ears was ripped along the seam. I felt another stirring of recognition. I had loved and cuddled this rabbit when I was little. I was sure.

'I see you found Baby Rabbit.' Annie was standing at the door, next to Shelby. I was struck by how they both had the same upper lip shape – full, and pointed in a V-shape in the middle.

I remembered the way my mother on the beach had laughed. Somehow I couldn't imagine Annie laughing.

She whispered something to Shelby, who scowled then scuttled off. Annie came inside and shut the door. She ran her fingers over a shelf of little board-books.

'I kept everything just as it was when . . .' she looked away.

I stood awkwardly, shifting my weight from one leg to the other.

'For years this was the only place I could be still. The only place I could find any peace,' Annie said. She walked across the room to where I was standing. Her fingers trembled as she touched my arm. 'Would you like to sleep here? We can go through all the baby things another time – decide what you want to keep.'

I nodded, then shrank back, pulling my arm away from her hand.

Annie stood there for a few seconds, her hand still outstretched. Then she turned and walked out of the room.

I sank down on the bed. Shelby was right. Annie didn't want me. She wanted the daughter she'd lost. She wanted eleven years of meals and cuddles and plasters on knees.

But she didn't want me. Here. Now. As I was.

And I didn't want her – I wanted the mother I had remembered. The woman I had dreamed.

I curled up into a ball and cried until I fell asleep.

29

The row

Several days passed. I was going mad trying to get news about Mum and Dad. Their lawyer drove me nuts. He was like the hardest person in the world to get hold of. Then, when I did speak to him, he gave only vague answers to my biggest questions.

When can I get out of here?

When can I see Mum and Dad?

Not that I was living in some hell-hole. Sam and Annie's house was far smarter and more glamorous than where I lived in London. But it wasn't home.

Missing Mum and Dad was this constant ache. It was strange. Considering how often I'd hated them when we were back in London, I would never have imagined I'd miss them as much as I did. I mean, it wasn't that I wanted to talk to them about anything specific. More that I wanted them there in the background, doing their Mum and Dad thing, alongside all the smells and sounds of my normal life.

After a week or so, I'd kind of settled into a routine.

After Shelby and Madison left for school, I'd get up. Then Sam and I would often go down to the marina. Sam had taken a month's leave of absence from his work. Annie says he's usually really busy, so the month off was a chance for him to unwind as well as to get to know me.

To be honest, I don't think he's massively into unwinding. That's why he spent so much time doing stuff on the *Josephine May*. Sometimes we'd go out, sailing round the bay. Those were my favourite times, especially when Madison came too. We'd stand in the bow, our faces pressed against the wind. And I'd forget about everything.

It's lovely when you get out there in the bay and look back at Evanport. The houses on the west side of the coast are all wooden-boarded and painted in pale pastel colours. Sam said they were really old, though they just looked like big beach houses to me.

Jam had somehow got hold of a video camera phone, which meant now we could send little videos and pictures to each other. We talked all the time. He knew everything. How miserable I was. How much I missed him. How desperately I wanted to come home.

When I wasn't calling or texting him, I wandered about on my own, exploring all the cafés and shops – stores, I should say. Annie and Sam gave me loads of dollars my second day. Told me to go out and buy some new clothes.

I got a new pair of jeans and several cute little tops, plus loads of this fabulous Ultra Babe make-up.

But my best purchase by far were these knee-length brown leather boots with high, spiky heels. I was dead nervous taking them back to the house. Mum would have had a fit if she'd seen me in them, but Annie just said how pretty they were.

MJ called most days, about lunchtime. She kept me up-to-date with the search for Sonia Holtwood, which was not going well. Unsurprising really. Sonia Holtwood was just one of a number of identities the woman used. She nicked them from people the same age as her who died when they were kids. Just thinking about it gave me the creeps. Anyway, so far the FBI didn't even know what her real name was.

Annie never tried to talk to me about Sonia, or Mum and Dad. In fact, by the end of my first week, we'd pretty much stopped talking altogether. Well, I'd stopped talking to her.

That sounds mean, doesn't it? But if you'd seen the way she acted, you'd understand. She was always hovering somewhere nearby, watching me all the time. Then she'd give this irritating little cough. 'Ooh, Lauren,' she'd say – all bright and chirpy. And off she'd go. Did I want more counselling sessions? Would I like to meet the rest of the family? When might I be ready to think about high school?

It was so fake.

I preferred being around Shelby. At least she and I knew we hated each other. But with Annie I felt like an itch she couldn't scratch. The more I drew away from her the more she hovered. The more I made it clear I didn't want to be near her, the more she grasped at me.

I could see Sam was anxious about the whole situation. But no one said anything and the tension between us built up and up. Then, two weeks to the day I'd arrived, everything came to a head.

I'd just been looking at *Goodnight Moon* with Madison. I'd found the book on the shelf in my room. I only had the vaguest memory of actually reading it when I was younger, and the pages were creased and dirty round the edges – but there was something strangely comforting about just holding it in my hand.

I sniffed in the dry, musty, deeply familiar smell of the paper while Madison learned some poem she wanted to do for Show and Tell the next day. She was laughing because she kept getting the words 'ants' and 'pants' muddled up.

Then Mum and Dad's lawyer, Mr Sanchez, phoned.

'Is something wrong?' I said.

'I do have news,' he said. 'Taylor Tarsen's out on bail now. And so are your adoptive mom and dad.'

'So can I see them?' I said eagerly.

'No. This is the problem,' he said. 'The Purditts are trying to block any kind of access visit. They are arguing there is a serious legal risk that your adoptive parents will attempt to abduct you if they are allowed to see you.'

'I'll speak to them,' I said.

I put down the phone, seething with fury.

Annie fluttered out of the kitchen. 'Any news, Lauren?'

I marched up to her. 'How dare you try and stop me from seeing my mum and dad.'

Annie blanched. 'Wait, Lauren,' she said. 'You don't understand.'

'They brought me up for eleven years,' I shouted. 'I have a right to see them.'

Sam and Shelby appeared from nowhere.

'They took you away from us.' Annie wrung her hands.

'They didn't know where I'd really come from,' I yelled. 'But even if they did, they're still my parents more than you are.'

'Don't speak to my mom like that,' Shelby snapped.

'Everyone calm down,' Sam said. 'Lauren, I know this is hard, but you have to face what they've done. They don't deserve to see you.'

'And what about me?' I shrieked. 'Stuck here for ever. I hate it here. I hate it. I hate it.'

I turned and ran up the stairs. I could hear Annie

pounding after me, Sam calling her to come back. I got to my room and slammed the door.

But there was no lock. A few seconds later Annie barged in.

'Get out,' I yelled.

'No.' Her eyes narrowed.

I swore at her.

She marched across to the bed and yanked on my arm.

'How dare you treat me like this,' she yelled, pulling me upright. Her face was completely red, her eyeballs bulging with fury. 'I have done nothing but tiptoe around you since you got here. I love you so, so much and you won't even let me in.'

'You don't love me,' I screamed. 'You don't even know me.'

We stood there, face to face, glaring at each other. I waited, hoping she would just walk away and leave me alone.

But instead she let out a long, slow sigh. 'I'm sorry,' she said. 'I shouldn't have shouted.' She paused. 'There's something I'd like to show you – please?'

Thrown by her change of tone, I followed her sulkily into one of the guest rooms. Annie walked over to a tall cupboard in the corner and opened the door.

'Those eleven years, while your Mom and Dad were enjoying you, I was doing this.'

I peered into the cupboard. It was overflowing with files and boxes of papers. Stacks of yellowing newspaper clippings and internet print-outs were piled on the shelves.

Annie reached in and grabbed a file at random. She pushed it towards me. I read the peeling sticky label: *Possible sightings of Martha.* It was at least three centimetres thick.

'Looking for you was all I did.' Annie said. 'I was obsessed. I neglected Shelby. I neglected Sam. We even split up for a while. In the end everyone was telling me to let go, that you weren't coming back. But I never gave up.' She turned to me. 'Maybe you're angry with us because you think we didn't try hard enough to find you?'

'No,' I said, honestly. 'I never thought about it like that. I mean, I know it must have been hard not knowing but—'

'Hard?' Annie stared at me. 'I was terrified the whole time. I couldn't eat, I couldn't sleep. I stopped *living*. Wherever I went I saw you. Whatever I did, nothing ever took away the terrible guilt that I hadn't protected you properly, that day.' Her lip trembled. 'The terrible fear.'

'But you can't punish my mum and dad for that.' Tears pricked at my eyes. 'They were desperate for a child. When they paid Sonia all that money, they didn't know I wasn't hers.'

Annie ran her hand through her hair. 'Hasn't it occurred

to you that if nobody was prepared to pay people like Sonia Holtwood the huge amounts of money they want, they'd have no incentive to steal children and sell them?'

She walked out of the room.

I sat down on the floor, stunned. I'd never thought about what Mum and Dad had done like that. A great wave of misery welled up through me. I put my face in my hands. Why was all this happening to me? It wasn't fair.

After a few minutes I felt a little hand patting my back.

I looked up. It was Madison. Her chocolately eyes were round with concern. 'Hey, Lauren,' she said.

She put her arms around me and hugged me. It was the first proper human contact I'd had in a fortnight. I squeezed her back, tightly.

'I brought something to show you,' she said, pointing to a slim album on the floor beside her.

I sniffed and tried to smile at her. 'What's that?' I said.

'My special photo album,' she said. 'Pictures of you. And some of me. D'you want to see?'

I nodded, wiping my face. Madison snuggled next to me on the floor and we looked through the album together.

The first few pages were all baby photos marked with my name and the date. I stared at them, my eyes filling with tears again. Here was the life I had lost. The life I had so longed to know about back in London.

'I wanted to show you earlier,' Madison explained.

'Mommy said I should wait until you were ready. Like she's waiting for you to meet Gramps and Granma. But I thought you'd like them. Look.'

She turned a few pages to another set of baby pictures. The lighting and clothes were different, but otherwise I looked similar – the same chubby face and brown hair. Wait. I looked more closely. 'I've got brown eyes in these,' I said.

Madison giggled. 'That's me. We look alike, don't we?' she said proudly. 'Everyone says we look like Daddy too.'

I looked at her. I could see the similarity between Madi and Sam. The same turned-up nose and smooth, olive skin. Did I look like them too?

I turned another page. This set of pictures showed Madison – no, this was me again – on a beach. I looked about three. There was a red plastic bucket in my hand.

It jogged something in my memory. From my hypnotherapy with Carla. 'My bucket,' I said, my heart suddenly beating fast. 'On the beach.' *That was where I played Hide and Seek with my mother. With Annie.*

Madison nodded. 'It's near here – Long Mile Beach. It's where you went missing. Mommy told me.'

She pointed to the bottom of the page.

I gasped. It was the woman from my memory. Her eyes sparkling, her arms wrapped around me.

'There's Mommy,' Madison said. 'Wasn't she pretty?'

I stared at the picture. It was weird, seeing the face outside my own head. Unreal, somehow. I tried to match the beautiful woman I was looking at with the reality of Annie's strained, lined face. The similarity was there. I could see that now, especially round the eyes. But, eleven years on, Annie looked like an old woman. No. Not exactly older. More like the ghost of the woman in the picture.

'Mommy said she went sad when you went away,' Madison said, tracing her finger down the picture. 'Why isn't she happy, now you're back?'

30
From the heart

The texts started the very next day.

I was trying out some new Ultra Babe eyeshadow (Emerald Shimmer, if you're interested) in the big family bathroom next to my bedroom.

Out of the corner of my eye I saw Madison peering round the door. I pretended not to notice her, expecting her to jump out at me any moment. *Surprise!* But all of a sudden she spun round, so she was facing into the corridor.

Two seconds later I realised why.

Shelby was there. She didn't notice me inside by the sink, but I could see the back of her yellow head as she moved closer to Madison in the doorway.

'*Pee-oo*, what's that smell?' Shelby said.

From all the giggling that followed I guessed she was with some of her snotty schoolfriends. One or two girls often came home with her after school. They'd spend hours prattling on about the boys they fancied or the latest lip injection they were trying to persuade their parents to let them have.

'*Pee-oo*, that smell's disgusting,' Shelby's voice rose in mock-horror.

More giggling. I shifted a little so I could see more clearly. Shelby was standing side-on to me now, holding her nose. Madison was shrunk up against the door jamb. There was this awful, blank look on her face. As if she was trying to pretend she wasn't there.

I froze, my eyeshadow brush still in my hand.

And then, before I could do or say anything, Shelby reached out and lifted Madison's little top. She lifted it right up, so I could see the whole of Madison's flat, white little belly. There was a cluster of little bruises down Madison's side. Some were a dark purple, others more faded and greeny-yellow.

'Shitty, smelly girls get punished,' Shelby sneered.

I held my breath, unable to believe what I was seeing.

In a single, deliberate movement, Shelby leaned across and twisted a knot of flesh just under Madison's ribs.

Madison flinched. Tried to pull away. But Shelby was too strong.

In one long stride I was there. I shoved Shelby in the chest. She stumbled back across the corridor, crashing into one of her stupid friends.

'Stay away from her,' I hissed. 'Or I'll make you sorry.'

I caught a flash of the friend, her mouth wide open. And Shelby herself, her eyes glinting like bullets.

Then I dragged Madison back into the bathroom and slammed the door shut.

I was breathing heavily, my hands shaking with fury. I looked down at Madison. She was leaning against the wall, her face half-turned away from me. Her neck and cheeks burned red.

I touched her shoulder. 'Are you OK?'

She stiffened, pulled away a little. I was itching to drag her downstairs and show Annie and Sam what Shelby had done – had clearly been doing for some time. *Evil, evil cow.* But I could see that kind of attention was the last thing Madison wanted.

'If she ever tries anything like that again you tell me.'

Madison just stood there, rigid as a pencil, her face convulsed with shame.

I went back to the sink. The eyeshadow brush was still clutched in my hand. My eye fell on the little pad of eyeshadow I'd been trying out earlier. I held it out to Madison.

'Would you like to try some on?'

She gave me the tiniest of nods.

I sat on the edge of the tub and scooped some of the glittery green powder onto the tiny padded stick. I held it up.

'This colour will go really well with your eyes,' I said. 'You'll look like a movie star.'

Madison took a step towards me. She watched the stick as I brought it up to her face. 'Close your eyes,' I said.

She did.

I smeared a little of the powder on each lid. 'Don't want to put on too much, though,' I chatted, 'or you'll look like Mrs Shrek.'

Madison giggled.

I added a dab of mascara after the eyeshadow. Then a slash of pale-pink lipstick. 'You're so pretty,' I said. 'In a few years you'll be fighting off all the boys in your class.'

Madison made a face. 'Boys suck,' she said.

I grinned at her, then spun her round so she could see herself in the mirror.

She didn't say anything, but this little smile crept across her mouth.

'Hey, let me take a video.' I whipped out my phone. 'Pose.'

Madison went through her repertoire of acting faces. Happy. Sad. Cross. Scared. And, her *pièce de resistance,* Madly in Love.

We both laughed. I felt a surge of love for her as she smoothed out her long hair and scampered out of the bathroom. Poor little kid. What chance did she have, with totally screwed-up parents and a sister like Shelby?

My phone beeped as I was packing up my make-up things into the cute little bag I'd bought the day before.

I flicked it open, thinking it was probably Jam, texting just before he went to bed.

I opened the text, totally unprepared for what I was about to see. One line. Three words.

SAY NOTHING BITCH

My breath caught in my throat.

Shelby. It had to be. I thought about marching into her room and slapping her silly face.

My heart pounded with fear. Anger.

Then I decided she wasn't worth it.

I deleted the message and slipped the phone back in my pocket. Apart from my hand shaking a bit, anyone watching wouldn't even have thought I was bothered.

31

The lecture

I stopped talking to Shelby altogether and found even more excuses to avoid being near Annie. When I wasn't phoning Jam, or Mum and Dad's lawyer, I spent most of my time on the *Josephine May* with Sam and Madison.

One day, Sam took me to meet his parents. Just me and him. I was dead scared beforehand. I mean, a few of Sam and Annie's friends had popped in and out of the house before now – they all gave me these guarded smiles, like I was some kind of bomb that might blow up in their faces. I didn't care about them. But Sam's parents were my grand-parents. My family.

Though I wouldn't have admitted it to Sam or Annie, I wanted to meet them. I wanted to know what they were like.

'Annie doesn't think we should push things,' Sam said. 'But your Granma and Gramps are desperate to see you.'

They lived in this big seafront apartment near the marina. It was all on one level because Sam's dad was in a wheel-chair. Apparently he'd had a stroke two years ago. When

I heard this, I got even more nervous. Suppose he couldn't talk properly? Suppose he looked weird?

In the end it was fine. He answered the door in his wheelchair and had me bend down to kiss his cheek.

'You sure turned out pretty.' His eyes twinkled. 'I'm your Gramps.'

I smiled. He looked just like Sam, only with grey hair and wrinkles. And he didn't look ill at all, except for maybe the way his right eye and right side of his mouth drooped down a bit.

Sam's dad backed up his chair and wheeled it fast across the big wooden hallway. He burst through the door at the far end.

'Gloria,' he yelled. 'They're here.'

'Thinks he's driving a racing car.' Sam shook his head, then walked after his dad.

I followed more slowly, suddenly shy of meeting his mum. She emerged through the door just as Sam reached it. She hugged him. 'Sammy,' she said. 'Thank you for bringing her.'

She peered over Sam's shoulder at me. She was tall, with the same nose as Sam and Madi, and dressed in an elegant, pale-green twin-set.

I stood in the large hallway while she disentangled herself from Sam. Her heels clacked against the wooden floor as she walked over. She stared at me for a few seconds. I felt this stirring of memory – like when I'd looked at Baby Rabbit. Her eyes were dark brown, deep and intelligent.

'You remember me, don't you?' she said.

She moved closer and pulled me into a hug. It was so quick I didn't even have time to tense up. And then I breathed in. A deep whiff of a flowery scent. And suddenly I was taken right back to being a little girl again. It was overpowering. Like my memory of the woman on the beach.

That scent meant being loved.

My heart beat faster and tears sprang to my eyes. Sam's mum hugged me tighter.

'It's OK, it's OK,' she whispered, rubbing my back. 'It's not surprising you remember me. I looked after you a lot when you were little.'

To my complete embarrassment tears were now leaking down my face. Sam's mum held me away from her and smiled. 'That's it,' she said. 'No shame in crying. Let it out.' She stroked my hair. 'Now I guess it'll feel a little odd to call me Granma straight off, so why don't you call me Gloria?'

I sniffed and nodded, wiping my face. It was weird. Though I hadn't wanted to cry like that, I hadn't minded her holding me at all. It had felt natural – like when Madison had hugged me.

Why wasn't it like that with Annie?

Gloria winked conspiratorially at me, then turned to Sam. He was staring open-mouthed at us.

'Close your mouth and spare the flies, Sammy.' She grinned. 'Lauren and I always did have a special connection. I told Annie it would be OK.'

She took my arm and led me into the living room – a huge open space with big glass windows right down one side of the room. Sam's dad had parked his wheelchair beside a long, low coffee table. He grinned at me.

Gloria sent Sam off to make some coffee. Then she sat me down on the couch beside her. 'Now,' she said. 'Just because we're related, doesn't mean we know anything about each other. So I want you to tell me about yourself. Start with the important things. Did you have a boyfriend back in Britain?'

I blushed.

Sam's dad chuckled from his wheelchair. 'That means yes,' he said.

'Well, go on,' Gloria said. 'Is he a dreamboat? That's what we used to call them in my day.'

I blushed more deeply. I couldn't believe these people were my grandparents. They were talking about boys and stuff like it was the most natural thing in the world. Yet they must be ancient. Sixty at least.

Gloria let out a peal of laughter. 'So. A dreamboat boyfriend. I guess you miss him, then?'

I looked through the long window at the sea. I nodded. Gloria patted my hand. 'And your mom and dad, from England?'

I gulped, nodding again.

'Tell me about them,' she said.

I looked at her. Her eyes were bright and enquiring. Kind – but not grasping like Annie. Like she wanted to know me. But she was confident it would all come in its own time.

I liked her.

I told her about Mum and Dad. She listened, not taking her eyes off me, just nodding every now and then. I talked and talked. About how everything they did used to make me angry. But how much I missed them now.

I told her things I hadn't breathed a word of to Annie and Sam. How the case against Mum and Dad was building up fast. How Mr Sanchez had told me that Taylor Tarsen had done some kind of plea bargain, which meant he would get a lighter sentence in court for giving up information on the other people involved in the kidnapping.

'And now he's saying that Mum and Dad knew about Sonia stealing me,' I said, the words tumbling out. 'He says they offered him money to organise all the phoney checks and adoption paperwork for them. But he's lying and I'm so worr—'

I caught sight of Sam heading towards us across the hall, a tray of coffee cups in his hands. I looked down.

Gloria pursed her lips, but said nothing. She squeezed my hand, then gracefully changed the subject to Sam's boat.

We drank our coffee, then got up to go. Sam had warned me that however well his dad seemed, he got tired very easily and needed to rest. While I was saying goodbye to him, I noticed Gloria whispering urgently in Sam's ear.

On the way home I wanted to ask him if she'd said something about me. But Sam was unusually distant – all wrapped up in his own thoughts. At first I wondered if I'd done anything to annoy him. Still, once we'd got home his mood seemed to pass. And by the end of the day I'd forgotten all about it.

The following day was a Saturday. It was the middle of November, two-and-a-half weeks since I'd arrived at the Purditts. I was feeling better than I had for days, really looking forward to talking to Jam about meeting my grandparents. It would be good to tell him something positive for once. Since the text from Shelby, we'd been calling each other several times a day and I'd started worrying he would get fed up with me going on and on about how miserable I was at the Purditts.

Not that he ever said anything. He was always brilliant. 'Hang in there,' he'd go. 'We'll see each other soon.'

I couldn't see how that was going to happen, but I just loved the determined way he always said it.

On this particular Saturday I was expecting him to call any minute. He usually texted early afternoon, UK time, when he knew I'd have just woken up. It was a beautiful day – the sun shining fiercely in a blue sky, the air all crisp and cold. Sam, Madison and I had come down to the marina – my favourite place in Evanport. Sam was keen to take me and Madison sailing one last time before the weather got too icy.

He'd stopped off at a store to buy a few things while Madison and I went down to the boat.

As Madison skipped on ahead, a huge shadow fell across my path. 'Lauren,' said a deep, gruff voice.

I looked up. 'Glane!'

He was standing in front of me, arms folded, looking hugely pleased with himself.

I guess it sounds crazy, seeing as I really hardly knew him, but starved as I was for friendship, I couldn't stop grinning. I threw my arms round him.

He hugged me, then held me out by the shoulders. 'I thought I would visit with you.' He beamed. 'So how is it?'

My lip trembled. I could see Madison ahead of me, looking back at us. I beckoned her over.

'Madi, tell Daddy I've gone to get a drink, OK?'

She nodded and ran off.

'Your sister?' Glane smiled.

I nodded and started walking back up to the little coffee stand on the jetty. Glane strode next to me, his legs taking one stride for every two of mine.

'So what is wrong?' he said.

I could feel the tears bubbling up behind my eyes. 'Everything,' I burst out. 'I have to live here with a family of people I don't know. Shelby's a total cow. Jam's thousands of miles away. I mean Sam's OK and his parents are nice but Annie's awful. And she and Sam won't even let me see Mum and Dad . . .'

My words dissolved into sobs just as we reached the little stand on the jetty. There was hardly anyone else about. Just a couple of smartly dressed Evanporters at one of the little tables a few metres away.

I took a table as far away from them as possible and waited for Glane. While he bought a black coffee for himself and a Diet Coke for me I remembered all the things he'd said about how hard it was for Jam being without his dad. As Glane set our drinks down I looked up at him, certain I would see sympathy in his eyes.

But Glane was frowning. 'I don't understand,' he said. 'You have found that you were a missing child. This is what you wanted, no?'

'Yes,' I said, the tears welling up again. 'But it's awful. I didn't want to be taken away from my family.'

'What *did* you think would happen?'

I frowned. The truth was that all the time I was trying to find out if I was Martha, I hadn't looked that far ahead.

'I just wanted to know the truth.'

Glane blew on his coffee, then took a swig from the styrofoam cup. 'Well. Now you have it.'

I leaned forward, trying to make him understand. 'But Mum and Dad might go to prison.'

Glane nodded. 'It is terrible, of course, that they are accused of this dreadful crime. But I met them – they are such good people. I am sure they will be cleared. It is just a matter of time.'

I could feel my temper rising. 'And meanwhile what about me? I have to live here with—'

'With your family,' Glane interrupted. 'The family you sought out, who lost you for eleven years. What do you think that was like for them?'

I glared at him. Why didn't he understand?

'But they don't know me. I don't know them. They even think my parents are guilty of stealing me when I was a baby. They expect me just to fit in, but I don't. I don't belong here. I want to go home.'

Glane glugged down the rest of his coffee. He stared at my Coke, which stood untouched in the middle of the table. He ran his large forefinger down the condensation on the side of the can.

'You are not seeing what is there, Lauren.'

‘What does that mean?’ I snapped. ‘I see perfectly. They wanted a toddler back and they got me.’

The people at the other table were staring at me. So was the man at the coffee stand. Out of the corner of my eye I could see Madison and Sam hurrying up the jetty towards us.

‘Lauren.’ Glane’s hand was warm and rough over mine. ‘I know it is hard. I do not say it is easy to be without your parents and your boyfriend like this. But it is hard for the family you have come into as well. Shelby – she is this other sister, no?’

I nodded curtly.

‘It must be difficult for her too – a pretty, older sister coming along just as she’s growing up herself.’

‘Believe me, she is a Class A—’

‘You have an opportunity here. To be part of another family. That is a rare blessing.’

I stared at him, not trusting myself to speak.

‘You have four parents who love you.’ Glane said. ‘For that, maybe it is possible to belong in two places.’

‘You OK, Lauren?’ Sam called out. He was pacing towards our table, an anxious look on his face.

Madison trotted up to me. She nestled against my arm, staring up at Glane with her big eyes. He smiled at her.

‘I just bumped into Glane,’ I said. ‘I’m ready to go now.’

And without looking at Glane again, I stood up and walked away.

32

The visitor

Normally I loved sailing. Standing in the bow with Madison, letting the salty wind tear past my face. But today it was all spoiled. I was deeply stung by Glane's words. How dare he suggest I was being selfish? I was in an impossible position, couldn't he see that?

To make matters worse, Jam didn't call. I couldn't get a signal out at sea, but once we got back home I tried to reach him several times. The phone only went to voice mail, and he didn't respond to any of my texts.

By the end of the afternoon I was cross. After what had happened with Glane I needed to speak to Jam more than ever. Why did he have his phone switched off?

But as the evening went on, I became more and more miserable. Maybe he'd got a new phone. But then why hadn't he let me know the number?

Maybe he'd got a new girlfriend.

My heart twisted with jealousy.

Shelby didn't help any by glaring at me all night either. I got another of her texts.

KEEP QUIET OR DIE BITCH

Another time this would have upset me a lot. But frankly, after the initial shock, I felt nothing but contempt for her. I wanted to phone Glane up and tell him, though.

See what she's like?

But I was too proud to do that. So instead I sent a text back to Shelby. It was a pretty short text – two words in fact. The second word was 'OFF'.

It didn't make me feel any better.

I couldn't sleep. Worry about Mum and Dad mingled with frustration at Glane and misery about Jam.

After two hours of tossing and turning I decided to make myself a cup of hot chocolate. I knew just how Annie did it. Two heaped spoonfuls of this delicious Chocolate Crème powder mixed with a bit of water, poured into a mugful of hot, frothy milk.

I padded down to the kitchen. I'd just whizzed up the milk with this little hand-held electric mixer thing, when I heard a noise outside the back door.

My blood ran cold.

The kitchen was a square room with windows down both sides and wide sliding doors out to the back yard at the far end. I looked towards the spot where I thought the noise had come from. I could make out nothing except the waving silhouette of trees against the night sky.

Reaching behind me, I turned off the light switch. As

the room plunged into darkness, a low, hunched figure scurried past the back door. My heart thudded. It looked too low to be human. But too bulky to be a cat or a fox. Maybe it was a bear. A small bear. Could bears get this far into a town? I had no idea.

The figure stood up. It was human. Hooded. I sucked in my breath, too shocked for a second even to cry out. And then, just as I opened my mouth to yell, the figure drew back his hood.

And smiled at me.

It was Jam.

The mug of frothy milk nearly slipped through my fingers. I set it down, then rushed over to the door. He was miming at me to get the keys and open the door.

I looked around. Mum always kept house keys hanging from marked hooks inside one of the kitchen cupboards. I didn't expect Annie to be that organised.

I pulled open drawer after drawer, trying not to make a noise, rummaging desperately among the lists and bills and catalogues that Annie clearly couldn't bear to throw away.

Nothing.

I looked round the room. Where would they be?

There. I saw them, lying on the edge of a bookshelf near the door.

My hands trembled as I fitted the three separate keys into the five different locks on the door. Jam was standing back, watching me. My hair was a mess. And I wasn't wearing any make-up. And had I even cleaned my teeth before I got into bed earlier?

At last I wrenched open the door. A gust of sharp, cold air. And then he was there, pulling me towards him. His hands cold on my face. His mouth warm on my lips.

Everything else fell away. He was here. He was with me. He was mine.

'What are you doing here?' I whispered.

He stepped inside and closed the door quietly.

'I couldn't stand it,' he said. 'You being so miserable and us being apart. I had to come back. So we could be together.'

I blinked at him. *But . . . but . . .*

Questions were flooding my head.

'How did you even get here?' I stammered.

'Two days ago Mum cancelled my phone. Said the bills were too expensive. It was kind of the last straw.' Jam shrugged. 'I bought the plane tickets using her online account. Then I nicked some money out of her purse, after she'd seen some clients that pay cash. I've saved most of it, though. The bus down from Boston was really cheap.' His face flushed. 'I know it was wrong, but I'll pay her back when I can.'

'Why didn't you call me?' I wound my arms round him. The sweetest feeling was sweeping through me. He had done all that to be with me.

Jam grinned – his cutest look. My heart skipped a beat.

'Thought I'd surprise you,' he said. Then his smile faded. 'This is what you want isn't it?'

I stared at him. 'Is *what* what I want?'

Footsteps creaked on the landing upstairs. I rushed to the kitchen door and peered round towards the stairs, motioning Jam to keep quiet.

We listened hard for a few moments. Then a toilet flushed and footsteps padded back across the landing.

Jam crept over to me. 'If we go now, we'll be miles away before anyone realises,' he whispered.

I blinked at him. A vortex of fear and excitement whirled up through my head.

'Jam,' I said, nervously. 'Tell me exactly what you want us to do.'

Jam frowned. 'Run away together, of course. Run away.'

33

On the marina

'But where will we go?' I said.

'I've got it all sorted out.' Jam ran his fingers through his hair. 'We'll head across towards the west coast. America's massive. We'll get lost in it. Find jobs. Rent an apartment.'

'But we're too young,' I stammered. 'And we don't have any money.'

Jam waved my objections away with a hand movement that reminded me forcibly of Carla. 'People have done it before. We can make it work, Lauren. If we've got each other, we can.'

I turned away and started locking up the door again.

Jam came up behind me and put his arms round my waist.

'You hate being here. And there's nothing for me at home. I mean, my dad isn't . . .' His voice cracked. 'And . . . and Mum doesn't care about me. She's more interested in her bloody spirit-flame candles.' He pulled me round to face him. 'If we leave tonight we can be miles away before anyone realises.'

My stomach churned. I wanted to go with him. But now was too soon. 'Not tonight,' I said.

'Why not?' I could hear the surprise, the suspicion in Jam's voice. 'Don't you want to get out of here?'

'Of course I do, but . . . but it'll be better if we have more money. I'm due my allowance tomorrow. Maybe I can ask for extra for something. Like an advance.'

Jam looked away. His eyes rested on the carton of milk I'd left by the fridge. 'What about me?'

'Come up to my room,' I said. 'You can hide there. Eat something. Rest.'

He nodded.

I grabbed the carton of milk and a loaf of bread from the kitchen, then led Jam up the stairs.

I held my breath as we passed Shelby's room, then Annie and Sam's. But everyone appeared to be fast asleep.

We slid inside my room and shut the door. Jam looked round as he pulled off his jacket. 'Kind of babyish, isn't it?' he whispered, stifling a yawn.

'It was mine – when I was little, remember?'

He nodded, then tore a chunk off the loaf of bread I'd brought up and popped it whole into his mouth.

I went over to the closet and pulled down a spare blanket off the top shelf. 'You'd better sleep in here. In case someone comes in in the morning.'

Jam swallowed his mouthful. 'I'm not tired.' He grinned. 'Hey. What about if I need to pee?'

I looked round. I grabbed a vase of fresh flowers Annie had put next to the board-books on the shelf. I pulled out the flowers and handed it to him. 'Use this.'

He raised his eyes, took the vase and disappeared into the closet. 'I'll be back in a sec.'

I paced up and down the room, my head spinning.

I wanted to be with Jam. I'd never wanted anything more in my life. Except . . . it felt wrong to leave Mum and Dad right now, while they must be so worried and scared about their court case. And for all that Annie annoyed me, was it really fair to put her through losing me again? And then there was Sam. And his parents. And, most of all, Madison.

After a while it occurred to me Jam hadn't reappeared from the closet. I wandered over. 'Jam?' I whispered. 'Jam?'

Silence. I peered round the door. Jam was sitting, slumped sideways on one of the cushions, his hand still clutching a chunk of bread.

I crouched down beside him and smoothed a strand of hair off his forehead. As I gently tugged him round onto the floor, his PSP slipped out of his trouser pocket. I picked it up and turned it over. Still six notches on the back.

How could his dad not want to see him?

For a second I filled up with how hurt Jam must feel. It made me sad. And angry.

I stroked his face again. Then I put a folded jumper under his head, covered him with a blanket and got into bed.

Madison often came in to see me in the mornings. Sometimes she'd bring me orange juice in a cup, sometimes a book to show me, sometimes a little bangle or earring that she'd made with one of her craft sets.

Today it was a picture she'd drawn. I could feel it, rustling against my hand as she shook me awake.

'Lauren, Lauren,' she whispered. 'Wake up.'

I opened my eyes.

Her face was centimetres away from mine. Her eyes like enormous buttons. 'Lauren, there's a boy in your closet.'

I shot up and stared over at the closet. The door was open. I could see Jam's feet poking out from under the blanket.

'I wasn't taking anything, just looking at your things,' Madison said, anxiously. 'I think he's asleep. Should we get Mom and Dad?'

'No,' I whispered. 'It's OK. Jam's a friend of mine. He got here last night. I . . . I didn't want to wake everyone up.'

'Is he your boyfriend?'

I looked down at the picture Madison had brought me. A crayon drawing of her and me standing next to each other in the bow of the *Josephine May*. 'Kind of,' I said. 'But he lives in England.' I looked up at her. 'He and I were thinking of going away. So it's important you don't say anything to anyone about him being here.'

'You won't go away for long, will you?' Madison's lip trembled. 'It's my birthday just after Thanksgiving and Mom wants me to have this big party, but I just want to go to the movies with you.' She leaned closer to me and whispered in my ear. 'You can choose what we see, if you like.'

I caught a whiff of her sweet, strawberry-jam breath. Fierce, protective love tugged at my heart. For a single, thrilling second I imagined Jam and me taking Madison with us. Then the image crumbled as I came face to face with its impossibility.

Which left me with one thought.

No way could I leave her.

'It's OK,' I whispered to Madison. 'We're just going down to the marina. You can come too.'

'What?' I hadn't noticed Jam coming out of the closet. He was standing at the foot of my bed. Madison shifted closer to me as Jam frowned and brushed back his tousled hair. 'What are you talking about?'

'Jam, this is Madi,' I said. 'She's my sister.'

Jam flashed her his big, cute grin. My heart flipped over. For a second I wavered. Was I mad even thinking about turning down the chance to run away with him for ever?

'We can't talk here.' I pointed to the clock: 9 am. 'There won't be many people down the marina. It's too cold. It's a good place to sort everything out.'

Jam's eyes lingered on my face, but he didn't say anything. He nodded. 'OK.'

It was easy sneaking out of the house. Madison stood guard at the bottom of the stairs while I led Jam through the living area and out the front door. I could hear Annie in the kitchen as we passed.

'An entire loaf of bread, Sam . . . You don't think she's bulimic?'

The marina was covered in frost. It crackled under our feet like a gigantic crisp packet. Jam and I walked without speaking.

As we reached the coffee stand, Madison skipped off by herself along the jetty. I watched her long black hair swaying behind her. There was hardly anyone about. A smart Evanporter walking a fluffy little Scottie dog. And a couple in the distance, both muffled up in hats and scarves. There was something vaguely familiar about the way the woman walked, but I was too preoccupied to give her a second thought.

The coffee stand was closed, but the iron tables and chairs, being nailed to the ground, were still in position. Jam and I sat at the same table where Glane and I had sat just the day before.

'So what's going on, Lauren?' Jam stared at me, his eyes hard. 'I went with you when you asked me. Why don't you want to come now?'

'I do,' I said. 'I want to be with you. I want that more than anything. It's just . . .'

My phone beeped. I ignored it.

'What then?'

'It's not that simple,' I said. 'Mum and Dad might be sent to prison for something they didn't do. I have to stay near them.'

'Why?' Jam frowned. 'Back in London you never stopped complaining about them. They drove you mad.'

'I know, but it's different now.' How could I explain? *I didn't know what it would be like to be taken away from them.* 'It's not just that. There's Annie and Sam too. They lost me for eleven years. I can't walk out on them.'

'But you kept saying how miserable you were here.' Jam turned away. The sun lit up a strand of hair over his forehead. He was so, so cute. And he wanted to be with me.

What was I doing?

My stomach twisted into a knot. 'Let me think about it.' I reached out and held his hand. It felt cold. 'Maybe

Annie and Sam will let you stay here. Once they know how we feel about each other.'

Jam pulled his hand away. 'Oh, grow up, Lauren. They won't want me barging in on their happy little family.' He stood up, just as my phone started beeping again.

I glanced down at it.

'Who's that? Your new boyfriend?' Jam snapped.

I didn't answer. I was barely even aware as he turned and walked away.

I was staring at the text on my cell.

Boat. Now. Or ur sister dies.

34

Finding Madison

Was it Shelby? Was this her idea of a sick joke?

I glanced across the marina. As far as I could see, it was completely deserted. So where was Madison?

Jam was still walking away from me. He had almost reached the point where the marina ended and the row of stores began. A few early-morning shoppers were strolling along the sidewalk.

'Jam,' I yelled after him. One of the shoppers stared at me. But Jam didn't look round. 'Jam. Please.'

For a second I stood, torn.

Jam was disappearing behind the first store: Tackle and Splice. 'JAM!' I yelled. 'PLEASE.'

My heart sank. I couldn't run after him. I had to find Madison.

I turned and raced down the jetty towards the boat. I was sure Shelby had sent the text. *Stupid, stupid cow.*

I muttered under my breath as I ran, vowing that when I got home I would personally go into her stupid closet and trample all over her stupid clothes.

I skidded to a halt beside the boat. It was eerily quiet.

'Madi?' I called out. 'Are you here?'

Silence.

I stepped on board. There was obviously no one in the stern. *Crap.* I was in my spiky-heeled brown boots. Sam would kill me for walking on the deck in these. I tiptoed past the saloon, up to the bow. I couldn't see anything through the windows. My heart thudded. Did Sam usually leave the curtains closed like that?

No one in the bow.

I crept back to the stern and over to the saloon door. The wood was splintered where Sam usually put the padlock. Someone had broken in. Would Shelby have done that?

I hesitated. Maybe I should run. Get help. But then I pictured the sneer on Shelby's triumphant face when it turned out the whole thing was a big joke.

Gritting my teeth, I pulled the door open and looked down the steps now in front of me. Immediately below was the place where all the maps and navigating equipment were kept. To the left stood the little galley – with its stove, mini-refrigerator and cupboards. Beyond the galley was the saloon – the main living space on the boat, complete with rugs and a couch and a TV.

I couldn't see into its shadowy corners. Not wanting to

turn my back on the darkness, I climbed down the steps front first.

'Shelby? Madi?'

My voice came out in a croaky whisper. There was no sound except for the water splashing gently against the hull and the creaking roll of the boat itself.

My mouth was dry. I crossed the galley and reached up for the light switch. I flicked it on. No light.

My heart pounded in my ears.

'If this is your idea of a joke, Shelby, I'll kill you.'

I took a step into the living area. At least I could draw back the curtains. Let some light in that way.

A scuffling noise in the corner. I whipped round. Was that the tip of a shoe? I stared into the darkness.

A shape loomed out of the shadows. A man. His face clenched with determination.

I opened my mouth to scream, but his hand, leather-gloved, was round my mouth and nose. He pulled me round, forcing my arm behind my back.

'Quiet,' he ordered.

He pushed me back through the galley, past the steps to the saloon door and aft, to where the main sleeping areas were. I struggled, but he gripped me tighter, wrenching my arm up. It hurt. I gave a muffled cry.

We were right at the back of the boat now. The man kicked open the door to the bigger of the two rooms.

He shoved me. I stumbled forward. Looked up.

There, slumped on the bed, her mouth covered with masking tape, was Madison.

Beside her sat Sonia Holtwood.

35

Links to a crime

Sonia's lips twisted into a cold, sneering smile. She had changed her appearance again – huge red curls tumbled heavily around her face, which somehow looked longer and thinner than before. 'Hi, Lauren,' she said.

I glanced over at Madison. She was struggling to sit up, but Sonia Holtwood kept pushing her back down onto the bed.

I felt a fury building inside me that completely drowned out my fear. I tried to go to Madi, but the man gripping my arm twisted it up my back again. I flicked my foot up behind me and jabbed the spiky heel of my boot between his legs.

'AAAGH,' he roared. He loosened his grip on my arm just enough for me to pull free. I raced over to Madison and yanked her to her feet. Then I turned, poised on the balls of my feet, looking for a way out of the room.

It was at this point that I realised just how hopeless the situation was. We were in the main bedroom, in the very deepest part of the boat. It was only a few metres square, with just enough room for a double bed, a closet and a washbasin. A tiny porthole high up in the wall, to the left of the bed, looked out over open water. Above the bed was a hatch, padlocked from the outside. The only other way out of the room was the door – which the man was standing in front of. He was bent over, clearly in agony from the stab of my high-heel.

The pulse of satisfaction I felt vanished as he straightened up, a look of total fury on his face. He walked towards me, his fist raised.

I pushed Madison behind me as he swung his arm back.

I flinched, closing my eyes, waiting for the blow.

It didn't come.

I looked up. Sonia Holtwood was standing in front of me, her hands on her hips.

'I told you, Frank – we have to make it look like an accident. No rope marks. No bruises.'

The boat creaked and rolled. Frank's nostrils flared. Then he dropped his arm. 'Fine.' He scowled. 'I'm going to start the engine.'

He strode out of the room. I could feel Madison's hand creeping into mine. I squeezed it, never taking my eyes off Sonia Holtwood.

She shook her head at me. 'Sit,' she said.

'What are you going to do with us?' I pulled Madison

down next to me on the far side of the bed and tugged the masking tape gently away from her mouth.

'Well,' Sonia said lightly. 'It's a question of priorities. As in, my priority of not being sent to jail.'

Madison huddled up close to me. As her body pressed against my side, I felt my phone through my jeans pocket. I looked up at Sonia. 'What do you mean?'

'I can't be sent to jail if I can't be identified,' she went on, 'and there are only two people who can actually identify me.'

'Me and Jam?' I shifted slightly, so that Madison was completely blocking Sonia's view of my pants leg. I reached my fingers into my jeans and felt for the slim edge of the mobile.

Outside, I could hear Frank's footsteps and the sound of rope slapping against the deck.

'Yes,' Sonia said. 'You and that boy. You see, they're after me for kidnapping you – twice – but nothing links me to the first abduction except the second, and nothing links me to the second except you two.'

I gripped the mobile and began easing it gently out of my pocket.

'My texts didn't seem to bother you,' Sonia went on. 'So I figured the next step was a little witness intimidation.'

My heart thudded. So the BITCH texts had been from Sonia, not Shelby, after all.

The phone was nearly out of my jeans now. I just had to keep her talking so she didn't notice it.

'How did you know my cellphone number?'

Sonia grinned. 'When you trade in identities, hacking into phone company records is a piece of pie.'

The mobile slipped in my sweating fingers.

'Identities?'

Sonia nodded. 'I make new lives for people. For myself, too. I can be anyone. No one can track me down.'

'What about Taylor Tarsen?' I gripped the phone more tightly. 'And all the paperwork on Sonia Holtwood?'

'Taylor's got nothing on me,' Sonia sneered. 'We've talked, done business – sure. But he only met me once, eleven years ago. Since then I've had a nose job and changed everything about the way I look. I doubt if he could pick me out of a line up. And I haven't used the "Sonia Holtwood" identity for years. Like I say, only two people can connect me to the whole thing.'

I pulled the phone fully out of my jeans just as the engine started to rumble.

There wasn't much time.

'Well Jam's not here.' I turned the phone round in my hand and felt for the tiny raised bump that I knew marked the number five. 'He'll still be able to identify you.'

'We'll catch up with him easy enough,' Sonia snorted. 'Why'd he walk off like that?'

I froze. She'd seen us earlier? And then it all fell into place. The couple I'd seen all muffled up in hats and coats earlier, on the marina. That was Sonia and the man, Frank.

'No reason,' I said, shortly.

The boat was moving now. A steady *chug*, *chug*, *chug*.

Sonia glanced out of the porthole.

I looked down at the phone. Bloody, bloody hell. No signal. I needed to get up on deck. Now.

Madison stiffened beside me. She was staring at the phone. I nudged her, trying to will her to look away.

'I feel sick.' I covered the phone with my hand. 'I need air.'

Sonia turned from the porthole. She pointed to the wash-basin in the far corner of the room.

'Use that.'

Clutching the phone to my stomach I walked over to the washbasin. I bent over and peered down at the phone. Still no signal.

I made fake retching noises into the sink.

The boat was moving faster now. I could feel the bob and swell of it, making the floor under my feet sway. Panic rose in my throat. The further away from shore we got, the less chance there was of getting a signal, even on deck.

'I still feel ill,' I said. 'Please let me get some air.'

'Stop whining.'

I stared at the video function on the phone. OK, so I

couldn't dial nine-one-one, but maybe I could get Sonia to say where they were taking us. Then, if I could somehow pass the phone to someone as we got off the boat . . .

It was a long shot, but it was all I could think of.

I bent over the sink again and switched the phone to video mode. I pressed record, then straightened up, leaving the phone on top of the plughole.

'Where are you taking us?' I groaned, still clutching my stomach.

'Shut up.' Sonia strode round the bed to the porthole and opened it. 'There. Now you've got some air.'

From the rush and slap of the water outside, I could tell we were cruising fast – but in what direction?

'My tummy hurts too,' Madison said from the bed. She curled over. 'It really does.'

'For Chrissakes!' Sonia opened the door and yelled down the corridor towards the saloon. 'Hurry up Frank, these kids are driving me mad.'

I looked at Madison. It was hard to tell if she was faking. She was holding her tummy and rocking backwards and forward on the bed.

I wanted to go to her, but I didn't dare either take the phone with me, or leave it behind in the sink.

Sonia moved away from the door, back to Madison.

'Stop it,' she yelled.

Madison curled her knees up to her stomach and wailed more loudly. She went on and on, piercing the air with her screams.

'SHUT UP!' Sonia's face was purple with fury.

Standing with my back to the sink, I scooped the phone up in my hand and held it against my side. Whoever found it – if anyone did – would need a picture of Sonia. As she said, no one except me and Jam – and now Madi – knew what she looked like.

My heart was pumping so hard I thought I might explode. I twisted the phone round, praying that I was holding it at a good angle.

Madison was definitely crying for real now. Sonia had hauled her up and was holding her by the shoulders and shaking her violently. A stream of swearwords exploded from her mouth.

'Stop it,' she shrieked.

Hoping I had enough footage, I slipped the phone back into the sink again and took a step towards the bed.

Madison's crying reached hysterical level. Then something seemed to snap inside Sonia. Her face hardened and set. She raised her hand.

Everything slowed down – like it was happening in slow motion.

I remember noticing Sonia was wearing thin, latex gloves. I could see the long red points of her fingernails through the tips. She drew back her hand, then drove it forward, hard, against Madison's cheek.

Madison flew across the bed. Her head smashed against the raised edge of the bedside shelf. She flopped down, her eyes shut.

Silence.

36
Crash

For a second which lasted a lifetime, I stared at Madison's limp body. Then time speeded up again. I rushed over to the bed. I brushed the hair off her face. 'Madi? Madi?'

Her eyelids flickered, but didn't open.

I could feel Sonia behind me, breathing heavily.

I turned, my hands outstretched, fingers curled over like claws, filled with a rage that came from the pit of my being.

Howling, I hurled myself at her. She caught my wrists and pushed me away, but I kept coming, screaming myself hoarse.

'You coward. You bully. You evil, evil cow!'

Sonia was forcing me backwards. She was far stronger than me. But at that moment I was madder than a lioness.

'She never hurt anyone. She's got nothing to do with this.'

Sonia finally pushed me away from her. I stumbled back against the closet and glared at her, panting.

Sonia adjusted her top and smoothed her hair.

'Your sister's fine,' she said. 'Look.'

There was a moan from the bed. Madison opened her eyes.

I rushed over to her and stroked her face. It was a ghostly grey-white. 'Just lie still, sweetheart,' I said. 'It's going to be all right.'

I turned to Sonia, who was watching Madison closely.

'Fine? Like my parents are fine?' I said. 'Going to prison for something they didn't do?'

Sonia shrugged and examined her nails under the latex gloves. 'Not my fault. Not my problem. I barely even spoke to your parents. I can't help it if Tarsen's a liar.'

The door burst open and Frank strode in. He took one look at Madison struggling to sit up on the bed and turned on Sonia.

'What the hell's going on?' he shouted. He glared at Sonia. 'Did you hit the kid?'

'It was an accident.' Sonia reddened slightly. 'Anyway, I'm paying you to be here. I don't owe you any explanations.'

'Jesus.' Frank rolled his eyes. 'You practically kill me for going to knock some sense into teen princess, and you can't even control yourself around the rugrat.'

'Don't have a cow. It'll just look like she banged her head in the crash. No one'll realise.'

'What crash?' I said.

Frank ignored me. 'I need you outside for this last bit,' he said to Sonia. 'You'll have to lock them in here until we're done.'

He went out. Sonia followed without looking back.

I heard the lock click in the door. The phone. I raced over to the sink. Thank goodness Sonia and Frank had been too busy yelling at each other to spot it.

I quickly ran to the porthole which Sonia had opened. Through it I could see the deck railings and open sea. But even holding the mobile up to the opening I could get no signal. Where the hell were we?

There was a coil of rope wedged up beside the porthole. I shoved the phone behind it. It would be safer there than on me. I could pull it out later.

I ran over to Madison and hugged her. 'You OK, babe?' I peered into her big brown eyes.

Madison gave a slight nod, then winced. 'My head hurts.'

She looked all right, but her eyes were a little glazed and her face still deathly white. Carefully, with trembling fingers I felt for where her head had banged against the shelf. She whimpered slightly as I touched something warm and sticky. I withdrew my hand. The fingertips were stained red.

Wiping the blood quickly on my jeans I smiled at her.

'You'll be fine,' I said.

'Did I do good pretending?' she said.

I blinked. 'You mean the tummy ache?'

Her mouth crinkled into a little smile.

I hugged her again. 'Good enough to win the best actress Oscar. Youngest winner ever.'

Bump. With a sudden jerk, the boat jolted us both forward, to the end of the bed. A screeching, scraping noise erupted from the bow. In the split-second that followed I wrapped my arms more tightly around Madison.

With a crash, the boat rammed against something hard and we were both flung onto the floor.

37

Trapped

I landed on my back, Madison on top of me. For a few seconds I lay there, winded. The boat was still juddering, though the engine had died.

Madison clung to me, whimpering. 'What is it, Lauren? What's happening?'

'I think we crashed.' The floor under my back was cold and hard. I gently eased Madison off me and scrambled to my feet. The boat was listing jerkily from one side to the other. I spread my feet apart, trying to keep my balance.

Footsteps padded along the corridor towards us. The door clicked unlocked and swung open. Frank was there.

'Don't want anyone to find you deliberately locked in,' he snarled. He turned and hurried back up the corridor, pulling a wetsuit jacket on over his T-shirt.

I dragged Madison after him, down the corridor to the saloon. The boat rocked and bucked. I leaned against the walls for balance, cursing my spiky boot heels.

Frank was climbing up, out of the saloon door.

No sign of Sonia. Then I heard her out on deck. 'Give

me her cell,' she shouted. 'We gotta leave it here. Don't want anyone tracing it.'

'I haven't got it,' Frank grunted.

Sonia swore at him. 'You were supposed to take it off her soon as she came on board.'

The boat bucked violently. I slipped to the ground, putting my hand out to save myself. The floor felt damp. *Oh God.* Water was seeping in, up through the floorboards.

'Lauren.' Madison was trying to haul me back onto my feet.

As I stood up, Frank reappeared on the steps.

'Where is it?' he yelled. 'Your cellphone?'

'I don't know.' It took all my concentration not to look back at the bedroom we'd just left. 'I dropped it on the marina, getting onto the boat. It fell in the water.'

Frank strode over. He shoved his hands in my pockets, then patted roughly down my arms and legs. He did the same to Madison. 'It's not on them,' he yelled up to Sonia.

The boat was moving less violently now. I looked down. Water was swirling at my feet. The toes of my boots were already stained dark brown.

'Leave it,' Sonia snapped. 'Let's go.'

Frank walked back to the steps that led up to the saloon door. Madison huddled closer to me.

'You can't leave us in here,' I shouted.

Frank said nothing as he climbed up on deck. The door shut, plunging the saloon into a shadowy gloom.

I could hear them outside, dragging something heavy across the deck. The water was up to the ankles of my boots now. I pulled Madison after me, wading towards the steps.

Something landed with a dull thud against the saloon door.

They've wedged something against the door. They want us to drown in here. They want it to look like an accident.

Panic rose in my throat. I hurled myself up the steps. The door wouldn't budge.

'Help,' I shrieked. 'Let us out.'

I hammered against the wood.

It was hopeless.

I looked back down at Madison. She was reaching up to one of the saloon windows, pulling back the curtain.

Through the tiny window I could see the boat was dangerously low in the water – close to an expanse of flat rock. A black and yellow pole topped with two black cones stood on the middle of the rock. In the far distance I could just make out a stretch of sandy beach.

'What's happening?' Madison's small, scared voice stabbed at me like a knife.

'It's going to be OK,' I said. 'They've just run us aground on some rocks.'

The boat's going to sink. We're going to drown.

Heart pounding, I looked round the saloon. There were plenty of windows, but they were all too small for us to climb through.

The boat gave a sickening lurch backwards. I gripped the grab-rail by the steps to stop myself falling off.

Madison slid into the water.

'Madi?' I yelled.

She stood up, dripping wet, her face crumpled with fear and misery.

I reached out my hand. 'Come on, Madi,' I urged. 'Maybe if we both push we can shift whatever's blocking the door.'

The floor of the saloon was slanting towards the stern now. Madison waded towards me. The boat rolled back again, sinking even further into the water.

How long did we have before we sunk completely?

38

The rock

I pushed again at the saloon door. It was totally jammed.

Madison was at the bottom of the steps, looking up at me. Her teeth were chattering. 'Daddy's g-gonna be m-mad about the boat,' she said. 'Lauren, my h-head really h-hurts.'

'I know, babe.' I thumped against the wood. 'Help,' I yelled, knowing it was hopeless. 'Help.'

I stopped. No response. Only the splash of the waves, the creak of the boat and my own, urgent breathing.

I thumped again.

Please. Please.

And then I heard it – an answering thump from outside of the saloon door. 'Lauren?'

My heart leaped. I hammered on the wood. 'Jam? Is that you? Jam?'

'Listen,' he yelled. 'They've wedged this boat hook between the door and the step here. I'm gonna pull it out.'

The scraping sound of metal against wood filtered through the door. I looked down at Madi. 'It's OK,' I said, tears of relief filling my eyes. 'Jam's here. He's going to get us out.'

I turned back to the door and pressed my palm against the wood. 'You came back.'

'Course I did,' Jam panted. 'I've been hiding down the back of the boat since Evanport.'

'Where's Sonia and that man?'

'All wetsuited up, swimming to shore,' Jam said, grimly. 'There.'

I heard the boat hook thud onto the deck. The saloon door opened. I caught a quick glimpse of Jam's face, then the boat gave a dreadful creak and jerked violently backwards again.

I was thrown off the steps and plunged into the icy water. For a moment everything was total confusion. Whooshing bubbles all around me. I whirled head over heels in the water. Sinking, I opened my eyes. The ignition panel was at my feet. I clawed at the water with my hands. Harder. Harder. Then my head broke through the water. Gulping in air, I looked around. Under the water, beside me, were the dining table and benches. The cupboard doors around them were all open. The water was littered with plates and cups that had been inside.

'Lauren.'

I looked up. Jam's head and shoulders were hanging down through the saloon door, now just a metre or so above the water.

He reached out his hand. 'Come on.'

I looked around. 'Madison. Where's Madison?' My voice rose in panic. I dived under the freezing water again. My clothes clung to me, making it harder to drag myself through the water.

I looked round. And then I saw her. Just a few metres away. Floating under the water, her long hair drifting out behind her.

My heart skipped about ten beats. *Madi, hold on.*

I pulled my aching arms through the water. It seemed to take for ever to reach her. Then I was there, hauling her up, up out of the water.

I was right under the open door, Madison a dead weight in my arms. Jam was leaning down towards me, his upper chest and arms completely through the opening.

'You'll have to push her up,' he said.

I shoved her out of the icy water, feeling Jam take some of her weight in his arms.

'Push her higher,' he gasped. 'I can't take her weight and keep my balance.'

I summoned strength from somewhere and with a mighty heave, thrust Madison's limp and sodden body towards him. Then she was gone. I trod water, making as little movement as possible. I realised that I could no longer feel my legs.

'Lauren. Lauren.' Jam was yelling my name.

I looked up. He wasn't far above me now. His hands were even able to reach the water. But it was too cold. What was he saying?

'Grab my hand, Lauren. Grab my hand.'

I looked, stupidly, along my arms. My hands were drifting listlessly in the water. It was an effort to move them. Even the small movement I was making with my legs took too much effort. It would be easier just to stop. Just to let the water pull me down.

'Lauren.' Jam's shout echoed round the watery room. 'Take my hand. Take it. Now.'

With a huge effort I reached out and let his hand grip my wrist.

'Now grab the door and pull yourself up,' he yelled.

I tried to make my arm lift up, but there was no strength left. The opening was only half a metre above my head, but it might as well have been half a mile.

'I'm not leaving you,' Jam yelled. 'D'you want me to die here? D'you want Madison to die?'

No. No. NO.

I reached up and somehow grabbed the saloon door. I gritted my teeth and told my muscles to pull me up. Jam's hands were under my arms, pulling me too. I hooked one arm onto the outside of the door. Then the other. I could feel Jam's hands, scrabbling over my back, pulling me upward.

And then I was there, clambering out into the cockpit, then onto the saloon roof, just a metre or so above the crashing waves.

The cold air hit me like a slap, but it was better than being in the water. I knelt, hunched over my knees, shivering.

'Get up,' Jam shouted. He was standing, barefoot, beside me, with one of Madison's arms slung round his shoulders. She hung from him, moaning lightly, all limp and floppy.

I struggled to my feet, trying to keep my balance against the rocking of the boat. It was sinking faster now. We didn't have more than a minute or so before we would be sucked completely under.

I took Madison's other arm and pulled it across my own shoulders. Jam pointed to the flat rock I'd seen out of the saloon window. 'We have to swim to that,' he gasped.

I nodded. The rock didn't look too far away, but the water around it was choppy. And I knew how cold it would be.

Together, we plunged into the water. Instantly my legs and arms grew stiff. Lugging Madison's weight between us made it even harder to drag our way through the waves that crashed round our faces. I could feel Jam pulling ahead, his arms and legs fresher and stronger. I struggled to keep up with him, the effort at least keeping some feeling in my limbs.

For some reason, once we were in the water the flat rock looked further away. Gripping Madison's hand I pushed myself forward. One stroke at a time. One more. One more.

My arms and legs were going numb again. Water splashed in my face. My legs knocked against lethal underwater jags, like the one that had torn the hole in the hull of the *Josephine May.*

Then, just as I thought I couldn't move any further, we were there. Jam scrambled onto the rock, half-dragging, half-pushing Madison as he did so. I hauled myself after him.

Jam's face was contorted with pain. I looked down. Blood was seeping through his trousers just above the ankle, running onto his bare foot.

'Cut myself,' he panted. 'One of the rocks.' He limped over to a pair of trainers which were lying on their sides in the middle of the flat rock.

How had they got here?

'They're mine.' Jam bent over and pulled a sock out of one of the trainers. He clamped the sock to his bloody leg and reached further inside.

My mouth fell open as he drew out my phone. I had forgotten all about it.

His face was blue with cold as he held it out to me. 'I saw you hide it. I'd have got to it earlier if I wasn't scared they'd see me.'

Shivering, I looked down. There was a signal. A faint one. My hand shook as I punched nine-one-one into the handset.

Jam was still talking. 'I wanted to call for help, but the boat was going down too fast. I threw it over here inside my trainer so it didn't get wet.'

A woman answered the call. 'Emergency services? Which service?'

'We're on a rock,' I stammered. 'In the water.'

'Where in the water? Where are you?' The operator's voice was brisk and efficient.

'I don't know where,' I said, desperately trying to focus.

'Somewhere called Long Mile,' Jam said. 'I heard them say.'

I told the operator. *Long Mile*. The name sounded familiar. But I was too cold and it was too hard to make myself work out how I knew it.

'How many of you are there?'

'Three.'

'Do any of you require urgent medical attention?'

Madison.

I shoved the phone at Jam and raced over to where she lay, face down on the hard rock. I touched her cheek. It was cold as ice. I turned her over and listened for a breath. Nothing. *No*. She couldn't be . . . I shook her hard. 'Madison.' A chill colder than the ice water ran through my blood.

'Madison!' I yelled. 'Wake up!'

39

Waiting

Through the gap in the curtains I could see doctors and nurses bustling past. The Emergency Room was noisy and busy but here, sitting up on my hospital trolley, I was outside the action.

Just waiting.

Waiting for news of Madison.

Annie and Sam had arrived about an hour ago – white-faced and upset. I'd seen them briefly – told them everything that had happened. I felt so guilty about Madison that I'd almost wanted them to get mad at me. To scream that I shouldn't have taken her with me to the marina that morning. That it would be my fault if she died.

But they just stood there, looking dazed. Then one of the nurses came by and took them off to the trauma room where Madi was being worked on. I'd wanted to go too. But the nurse said I had to wait to see the doctor again.

Now MJ had turned up and was sitting beside me. I tried to focus on what she was saying.

'Sonia Holtwood wanted to make it look like an accident

– like you and Madison had taken the boat without permission, then lost control and run it aground on the rocks.'

Please let her be all right.

MJ leaned forward. 'It was clever,' she said. 'Picking Long Mile Beach. You know, where you went missing.'

I stared at her, remembering the beach I'd seen in the distance when we were on the rock. And the photos Madison had shown me. 'Long Mile?'

MJ nodded. 'I guess Sonia thought it would look like you were going there because you were curious about it. I've handed over your phone video. At least now we have a proper picture of her. And we know she's in the area. We're going to get her this time.'

I nodded numbly. *What does it matter? Catching Sonia Holtwood won't help Madison.*

MJ left. I sat there, staring at my hands, reliving the last couple of hours.

They had winched us off the rock by helicopter. I guess that sounds exciting. But it wasn't. Just cold and frightening.

Madison didn't wake up all the time we were on the helicopter. The paramedics put these silvery cloaks round me and Jam to warm us up, and one of them checked out the cut on Jam's leg.

They kept looking at her, then at each other. They didn't say anything much in front of us. But I could see in their eyes they didn't hold out much hope.

'Lauren, did you hear me?'

Annie was right beside me.

I gripped her arm. 'Is she all right?'

Annie shook her head. 'No, she's still unconscious.' Her eyes filled with tears. 'Hypothermia, because she got so cold in the water.'

I should have protected her more. It was my fault she was even on the boat. Why had I taken her with us to the marina?

I opened my mouth to tell Annie that I was so, so sorry for all of it. But she was staring at the covers on my bed, a tear tracking its way down her cheek.

'At least you're all right Lauren,' she sobbed. 'I couldn't bear it if it was both of you.'

The sight of her standing there, hunched and miserable, wrenched at me. I wanted to say something comforting. But the words crumbled in my mouth. And then Annie left and a doctor came in to examine me. She said I was basically OK, but should stay overnight for observation. Which was fine by me. If Madison was here, there was nowhere else I was going.

Two more terrible hours passed. The doctors let me get up so I could wait with the others in the family room. There was still no news of Madison.

I sat huddled in one of Annie's jumpers in the corner of

the sofa. Shelby was curled up in the chair opposite. Annie stared out of the window, watching for Sam to come back. Impatient with waiting, he had gone to the trauma room again.

The door opened. Jam came in wearing a pair of Sam's trousers and a sweater, all rolled up at the arms and legs. He limped over and sat down beside me. We didn't speak. There was no need.

I leaned against his shoulder and closed my eyes.

I couldn't imagine loving anyone more, ever.

Except maybe my baby sister.

Every time I thought about her lying on that rock, her big eyes closed and still, I felt this crushing weight on my chest, like I couldn't breathe. Her voice echoed round my head – quiet and serious. I could see her smiling that first time I put my make-up on her.

Why are the doctors taking so long? Either she's all right, or she . . . No, she's all right. She has to be. I'm taking her to the movies for her birthday.

I only realised Sam had walked in when Annie dashed across the room to the door.

'Sam?' She caught her breath in a sob. 'Sam?'

Sam shook his head. There was this terrible emptiness in his eyes. 'No change yet,' he said. His face crumpled as Annie drew him towards her. He leaned his forehead down onto hers and wept.

I turned away, nestling further into Jam's shoulder.

Please don't let her die. Please don't let her die.

The guilt was swallowing me. And the fear.

If Madison died, part of me would die forever too.

Was this what being a mother felt like?

Sam stopped crying and sat down in one of the chairs. He ran his hands distractedly through his hair. 'The doctor said there were these little bruises on Madi's stomach. Old ones. Nothing to do with today. They were wondering if we knew anything about them.'

Annie shook her head. 'Maybe from some sports thing,' she said vaguely. She frowned. 'Though the last few months she's been very funny about bathing and getting dressed on her own. I thought it was just her trying to be independent.'

I caught Shelby's eye. She looked horror-struck. Her eyes pleaded with me not to say anything. I looked down. If Shelby felt half what I felt, she was suffering enough already.

There was a smart rap on the door. Annie jumped up. But it was only MJ. She beckoned me towards her. 'Lauren, can I have a word?'

I stepped outside the family room, back into the noise and bustle of the ER. MJ smiled. I frowned, dully, not seeing at first why she was looking so pleased. Then she glanced sideways. I followed her gaze and saw them. Mum and Dad. Standing there. Looking at me.

A lump filled my throat as they walked up.

'Are you . . . is it over?' I said.

Mum nodded. Her face was gaunt, her cheekbones pressing so hard against the skin that she looked more like a skull draped with flesh than a human being.

'We're free,' Dad said. His mouth trembled but he was trying to smile. 'All charges dropped. They're not even going to prosecute over the illegal payment to Sonia Holtwood.' He paused. 'We came straight here. I know the Purditts don't want us to see you. But we're going to fight them for you. We've filed what's called a Hague petition . . . Anyway, never mind the details. The important thing is it'll be easier now, without the criminal case hanging over us.'

'It was your phone video,' MJ grinned. 'Well, not just that. Tarsen kept changing his story and there was nothing to back any of it up. But the cellphone was kind of the last straw. They've thrown out the case against your mom and d—'

'I know the doctor says you're OK, but are you sure?' Mum interrupted anxiously.

'I'm fine, Mum.'

'We want to take you home,' she said shakily. 'But we know it won't be straightforward.'

'We'll work it out,' I said. 'I promise.'

As I hugged Mum's frail body, I was suddenly overwhelmed by this fierce desire for my old life in London.

I wanted to be back there. At home with Mum and Dad and Rory. I wanted it so badly I could hardly breathe.

Then I remembered Madison.

I turned and looked back at the family waiting room.

Annie was standing at the window, watching me, her eyes full of tears.

Mum and Dad went off to a hotel, to get some food and rest.

Jam phoned Carla. He told me seeing Annie and Sam get so upset about Madison made him feel guilty.

'I guess I should at least let her know I'm all right,' he said.

Carla was predictably furious with him – you could hear her on the other end of the line, shouting, from across the hall. Then Sam took the phone. He must have been feeling like crap, but he listened to Carla rant and gradually calmed her down, telling her how Jam had saved our lives.

After an hour or so, the doctors let us see Madison. She still hadn't woken up. Her head was bandaged and there were all sorts of tubes and wires sticking out of her. She looked so small, so vulnerable, lying on the bed, my heart seemed to shrivel up.

We took it in turns to sit with her.

Jam had gone off with Sam and Shelby to get some food. Annie and I sat on either side of Madison, each holding one of her hands.

It was dark outside the ICU window and the pole holding her drip cast a long line of shadow across the floor. We sat there for a long time without speaking. The only sounds were the muted voices of the nurses, busy with another patient across the room, and the occasional *beep beep* of a machine.

'It was like this when you disappeared,' Annie said.

I glanced at her. 'How d'you mean?'

'That day at the beach. It was just you and me. We were so happy. We played Hide and Seek. And then . . . then you ran behind these rocks where I'd hidden earlier. And when I got over to you, you'd disappeared.'

'I remember.'

Annie looked across the bed at me.

'Being taken by Sonia Holtwood, you mean?'

'No.' I met her gaze. 'I remember being with you on the beach. I remember playing Hide and Seek. I remember being happy.'

I looked down at Madison's hand.

'Letting go,' Annie whispered. 'It's the hardest thing.'

As she spoke, one of Madison's fingers twitched, slightly.

I gasped. 'Annie, look.'

I held my breath and squeezed Madi's fingers, willing them to move again.

They did. The tiniest, gentlest pressure.

'Madison?' I whispered.

'Mmmn,' she moaned softly. Her eyelids flickered. 'Mommy?'

I looked up at Annie. Her eyes were shining.

For the first time I saw her properly.

The woman on the beach.

My mother.

40

Decisions

They caught Sonia Holtwood trying to cross the border into Canada on Thanksgiving. MJ phoned and told me – said she was likely to spend a long time in prison. Apparently Sonia Holtwood (real name: Marcia Burns) had been involved in a series of child kidnappings before moving into internet fraud, developing and selling of stolen identities for people. She gathered together the information, then passed it to Taylor Tarsen to sell.

Jam and I would have to be witnesses at their trial. But, otherwise, the whole business was behind us.

Jam had been staying at Annie and Sam's since the boat crash. He got on with both of them really well. Even while Madison was still in hospital, they tried to shower him with presents.

'You saved our daughters' lives,' Sam said. 'Whatever you want, you've got.'

I think he expected Jam to ask for computer stuff – or maybe even a car. You can drive when you're sixteen over here. But Jam just looked him straight in the eye and said: 'I want to stay with Lauren.'

I think Annie and Sam were a bit shocked but, to be fair, they got straight on the phone to Carla and persuaded her to let him stay until the end of November. She insisted he did a certain amount of schoolwork everyday, but otherwise she didn't put up much of a fuss.

To my surprise, Mum and Dad didn't seem to mind Jam staying with the Purditts either. I guess they were just so happy not to be going to prison that nothing could upset them.

They moved back into the Evanport Hotel for a few days, then went home for a week to see Rory. I bought him a *Legends of the Lost Empire* T-shirt and asked them to give it to him. I reckoned I owed him that much for ruining his holiday.

The hearing to resolve where I was going to live would begin when they came back. I was dreading it. I mean I wanted to be with Mum and Dad, of course. But I also wanted to be here, with Annie and Sam and Madison. And I couldn't bear the thought of another court case. Especially one with me in the middle of it.

I told Gloria how I felt. The next day Sam and Annie sat me down in the kitchen for a Serious Talk.

'What is it?' I said.

Annie gave a nervous little cough. 'We just wanted to discuss about this legal situation we've gotten into.'

I stared at her.

'Sam and I realise that we were wrong about your . . . your adoptive mom and dad. I mean, we know they were basically good people who thought they were helping when they paid Sonia for you.' Annie took a deep breath. 'Once the hearing next week establishes your adoption was illegal, they'll be able to start fighting to get you back. Our attorneys say they have a strong case. And we . . . we understand how much it means to you to see them, and so we want to try and work things out without a big legal fight and . . . and see if there isn't some way that you could spend time with them too . . .'

I flung myself at her, burying my face in her neck, squeezing her tight.

'Oh, Annie, thank you, thank you.' I hugged her again.

'Well, it was Sam too.' She looked somehow pleased and sad at the same time.

I glanced at Sam.

'Actually it was Mom. My mom, I mean. Gloria.' He grinned. 'She pointed out to me the day you met her that it wouldn't matter if the people you called Mom and Dad were mass-murderers. You were always going to see them as your parents. And Annie and I somehow had to come to terms with that.'

I thought back to that first meeting with Gloria, and how preoccupied Sam had been on our way home.

I beamed at him, then at Annie. Her lip trembled and I felt a pang of guilt for how often I'd been mean to her in the past. I wanted to say something – about how hard I could see it was for her and Sam to realise I thought of other people as my parents. About how confused I was about where I wanted to live and who I wanted to live with.

But I couldn't find the right words – so I just got up and went to look for Jam. At least with him it was straightforward. At least with him I could forget how torn I felt – for a while, at least.

Madison came out of hospital in time for her birthday at the end of November. Annie wouldn't let her go out to the movies, so I bought her *ET* on DVD and we watched it in her room, crying together at the bit when ET seems to die so that Elliot can live.

Jam came in, saw us weeping, and groaned. 'That's the trouble with chick-flicks,' he said. 'Way too mushy.'

I told him *ET* wasn't a chick-flick, while Madison pestered him to stay and watch it. Between you and me I think she's got a little bit of a crush on him.

ET finished and Annie made Madi lie down for a nap. Jam and I wandered down to the marina. It was always deserted now, all the boats covered over with tarpaulins for the winter.

We held hands and made out for a bit. But it was all overshadowed by the fact that it was almost the end of November and Jam was going to have to go home in two days. Suddenly it struck me that Annie and Sam's vague offer of sharing me with Mum and Dad wasn't enough.

I wanted to be with Jam all the time. Not just when Annie and Sam felt like letting me go home.

Why did it have to be so complicated?

'Maybe we could run away after all,' I smiled, wrapping my arms around him.

'Nah. You were right about that. Anyway, I guess you belong here now.'

I snuggled against his chest. Did I belong here? I was never going to feel that Annie and Sam were my mum and dad, but I had started thinking of them as family. And since last week, Shelby hadn't been rude to me once. To my utter amazement she'd even fessed up to bullying Madison.

Annie put what she'd done down to the trauma of having a missing sister. I put it down to Shelby having a serious attitude problem.

Still.

I guess she did seem to be changing.

A blast of icy wind whipped off the marina, chilling my neck. I tugged at my scarf.

So where *did* I belong? I didn't particularly want to go

back to school in London, but I missed Mum and Dad. I knew they wanted me to be with them properly, not just on occasional visits. And how was I going to say goodbye to my totally amazing boyfriend?

I stretched up and kissed him on the nose.

'I want to be with you.'

He gave me his big, cute grin. And there wasn't much more talking for a few minutes.

The whole family came round later for Madison's birthday tea. I'd helped make a big cake with seven candles. Madison blew each one out in the manner of one of the seven dwarfs from *Snow White*. Only Jam and I guessed what she was doing. We creased up at Annie's face when Madison, as Sneezy, manufactured a massive sneeze to blow out the last one.

Then everyone left. Sam took Madi up to bed and Annie cleared up. She seemed particularly on edge, breaking a plate and two glasses as she loaded the dish-washer.

I wondered what was wrong. In the past few days Annie had seemed calmer than before. She'd even stopped creeping around me all the time. But tonight she was definitely jittery as hell.

At seven o'clock the doorbell went. Annie jumped like she'd been shot. 'Lauren, would you get that?'

I trotted across to the front door.

Mum and Dad stood on the mat outside.

My mouth fell open.

'Hello, sweetheart.' Mum drew me into an enormous hug.

'What's going on? I thought you weren't due back until tomorrow.'

'Annie and Sam invited us.' Dad raised his eyebrows, as if to say 'we've got no more idea than you do'.

We went through to the living area. Sam and Annie were standing there looking ultra-serious. Mum and Dad stared at them. I caught Jam's eye. This was by far the most bizarre situation I think I'd ever found myself in.

No one said anything.

I cleared my throat.

'Er, Mum and Dad, this is . . .' I turned to Sam and Annie. 'This is . . . er . . . my mum and dad.'

Jam laughed. Everybody else looked awkward.

Sam held out his hand. 'Thanks for coming,' he said.

Mum and Dad sat down on the sofa opposite Annie and Sam.

'I'll make some coffee in a minute,' Annie said. 'But I think if I don't say this now I'll burst or cry or something stupid.'

I stared at her.

Sam coughed. 'First off, we wanted to apologise for ever believing you were involved in Lauren's kidnapping. We know that you did . . . er . . . what you did, thinking you were saving her.'

Annie nodded. 'And we want you to know that we think you've done a wonderful job as her parents. She's a lovely girl.'

Mum gave a half-smile. 'Thank you,' she said. 'And thank you for what you told Lauren and our lawyers about not fighting to keep us out of Lauren's life altogether. Knowing that you understand . . .' Her voice faltered. 'Is that what you wanted to talk about?'

'Not exactly,' Sam said. 'We know that you love her very much and we've talked to Lauren. It's obvious she feels she belongs with you . . .' Sam's voice croaked. He stopped and looked down.

Annie squeezed his hand. She looked at me. 'When I saw your face . . . the way you lit up when we told you we weren't going to fight you seeing your . . . your parents, I – we realised . . .' She took a deep breath and looked over at Mum and Dad. 'We wanted you to be here when we told Lauren that . . . that if it's what she wants, once the hearing establishes the earlier adoption was invalid, we won't fight your application to formally adopt her, legally this time, and have her go back home to England.'

I gulped. Glanced over at Mum and Dad. They were both staring at Annie and Sam. Mum's eyes filled with tears.

No one spoke. My heart thumped loudly in my ears.

'Thank you.' Mum's voice was a whisper. She looked at Dad. He nodded.

Mum cleared her throat. 'It's up to you, Lauren. We know finding your birth parents meant everything to you. It's your decision. Whatever you decide, we'll support it.'

What?

They all looked at me. I blinked rapidly. I could choose? I felt Jam's arm round my shoulder.

Mum and Dad meant rows and school and boring England. But it also meant being with Jam. And it was home.

But how could I leave Annie and Sam's? I hadn't spent enough time here yet – with my family. I wanted to get to know Annie better. And my grandparents. *Jeez.* I had relatives I hadn't even met yet. And I wanted to go sailing with Sam again when he got his new boat. And, most of all, I wanted to be here for Madison.

I gazed round at my parents' anxious, tearful faces. Glane's words came into my head.

You have four parents who love you. For that maybe it is possible to belong in two places.

A slow smile spread across my face.

'I don't want to choose,' I said.

They all stared at me. Dad cleared his throat. 'We don't want to make you,' he said. 'But we have to . . .'

‘I mean I don’t want to choose *between* you,’ I said. I looked at them, grinning.

Mum and Sam were frowning. Annie sniffed. ‘But how . . . ?’

‘Don’t you get it?’ I said. ‘I choose all of you.’

And that’s how we worked it out. I’m probably the first person in the history of the world with four legally recognised parents across two continents. I spend school terms at home in London, and at least half the holidays in Evanport. Annie and Sam and my sisters come to England for holidays sometimes too.

Jam and I are totally an item. I see him all the time at home in London – and he often comes with me to Evanport too. Sam pays for the flights. Jam still doesn’t see his dad and, well, he’s never got on with Carla. To be honest, I think he looks on Annie and Sam as substitute parents. Sometimes Glane pops down from Boston and takes us out too.

So that’s how it is. I never spend more than a few weeks at a time away from either of my families and we talk and text loads too. It doesn’t leave much time for other stuff and it isn’t always easy, especially when I’ve just arrived somewhere, but all in all I probably get on with everyone better than I would if I lived with them full-time.

We got a new teacher the other day. She made us do

one of those *Who am I?* essays again. This time it was easy. I just wrote about my life.

About me.

Girl, found.

Acknowledgements

This story started with the internet, in particular: www.baaf.org.uk (the website of the British Association for Adoption and Fostering), www.missingkids.com, www.ukadoption.com and Vermont Statutes Online at www.leg.state.vt.us/statutes.

I am especially grateful to Julia Alanen, supervising attorney for the international division of the US National Center for Missing and Exploited Children, for her time and her interest.

And thanks, also, to Elizabeth Hawkins, Moira Young, Gaby Halberstam, Julie Mackenzie, Sharon Flockhart, Melanie Edge, Jane Novak, Alastair McKenzie, Pam McKenzie and Ciara Gartshore.

If you enjoyed

GIRL, MISSING

Look out for the thrilling sequel,

SISTER, MISSING

**Turn the page for
an exclusive extract...**

Fighting back my rising panic, I stopped and took a deep breath. Think. Where could she have gone? I turned right around, looking in every direction, trying to spot the familiar silhouette of my little sister. But there was no sign of her.

Heart pounding, I grabbed the arm of a mother walking by, her baby in a sling.

"My sister's missing," I said. "She's eight-and-a-half."

"Oh." The woman's eyes widened. She raised her hand protectively over her baby's head, as if to shield her from the news. "I'm . . . er . . . that's terrible. What happened?"

"She went to buy an ice cream and she hasn't come back." As I spoke, my eyes scanned the beach again, desperately hoping I'd catch a glimpse of Madison in her denim shorts and blue t-shirt.

"When?" the woman asked.

"Not long. A few minutes ago," I said.

The woman's face relaxed. "She's probably just gone in the wrong direction. Got lost, not paying attention to where she was—"

"No." I shook my head. "Madison isn't like that."

The woman with the baby took a step away from me. Her expression registered sympathy but distance. She didn't want to get involved. "I'm sure your sister will turn up," she said. "Have you tried the Ladies?"

"Yes." The word snapped out of me. I spun around, searching the beach again. "D'you know if there's a life-guard here?"

The woman shook her head. "Not on this stretch, sorry." She walked off. I looked along the path after her and my breath caught in my throat.

Two Twisters, still in their wrappers, were lying on the tarmac, melting. Were those the ice lollies Madison had just bought?

I took a step towards them. Gasped. Just beyond the Twisters lay Madison's pocket doll, Tammy. She was face down on the ground, her shoes missing and one of her plaits untwisting in the sunshine.

And that's when I knew.

Madison hadn't wandered off, or gone in the wrong direction by mistake. Something really, really bad had happened.

I picked up the doll and shoved it into my straw bag. The world spun inside my head. I had to act. I had to do something . . .

I strode off across the sand. It was warm and soft, hard to walk in. Earlier I'd enjoyed the way the grains trickled up between my toes but now it was awful not being able to move faster.

"Mo!" I yelled as I hurried along. "Madison!"

Maybe she just dropped the doll. Maybe she got lost, I muttered under my breath, trying – and failing – to reassure myself. *Please, Mo.*

Surely she would appear any second – plaits streaming out behind her as she raced towards me.

But she didn't.

I headed for our two towels, still lined up on the sand, just a few metres from the sea. The whole area was busier than it had been even just a few minutes ago and I knew I was never going to spot Madison in the crowds. Hoping against hope, I called her again, but her mobile was still switched off. I held my phone in my hand – in case she called me – as I stopped to work through my options.

I knew I had to tell Annie. I didn't want to, but short of contacting the police I couldn't see what else to do. I glanced around, forcing myself to focus on every detail.

Please be here, Mo. Please.

Up on the promenade a group of teenagers were chatting outside the Boondog Shack. The boy who'd spoken to me earlier was with them. He'd obviously found the girl *he'd* been looking for.

Families were still swarming onto the beach. Shrieks and yells filled the air. There were plenty of little kids . . .

toddlers in sunhats waving toy plastic spades, a pair of skinny redheads in matching Bermuda shorts . . . an overweight girl about Madison's age wearing a bright pink dress.

I stood, trying to see everything all at once. It was no good. Panic rose inside me, whipping up through my body like a tornado.

And then my phone beeped. A text from Madison's phone. Relief surged through me. With trembling hands I opened the text.

Stop looking on the beach. Your sister isn't there. Do NOT contact the police or I will kill her.

SOPHIE McKENZIE

Madison's tracked down her real father
– but is he all that he seems?

@ sophiemckenzie_
www.facebook.com/sophiemckenzieauthor
www.sophiemckenziebooks.com

SOPHIE McKENZIE

The sinister Aphrodite Experiment
is underway – will Rachel have to pay
the ultimate price?

@ sophiemckenzie_
www.facebook.com/sophiemckenzieauthor
www.sophiemckenziebooks.com

A Q&A WITH THE AUTHOR

When did you realise you wanted to be an author?
In some ways I've always wanted to be an author – I certainly enjoyed writing stories when I was a child. However it took a long time before I felt confident that I had a story worth writing.

So when *did* you start writing?
Several years ago, I got made redundant from my job and decided to do a creative writing class to cheer myself up. Within a month I'd realised two things – firstly, I loved writing stories and wanted to carry on doing it for as long as possible and secondly, I wasn't nearly as good at it as I needed to be. I worked very hard for the next year or so – and eventually wrote *Girl, Missing* . . .

You've written lots of books – do you have a favourite?
Sister, Missing had to be my favourite! It was so much fun to revisit Lauren, Jam and Madison and find out how they were all doing, two years after the end of *Girl, Missing*. It was a challenge to write, though very rewarding, because the first book has been so popular and I wanted the second to live up to it.

Why do you write for teens?
I don't know. To be honest, I'm really writing for myself when I write a story. I do remember very clearly what it felt like to be 14 or 15, so maybe that explains why I gravitate towards teenage characters.

Do you prefer writing stand-alone books or series?

Series are more fun, simply because once you've got to know the characters you don't have to say goodbye to them.

Which authors inspired you?

Too many to list here. My favourite all-time author is Jane Austen, but I love loads of others. When it comes to contemporary writers, I'm a big fan of Anne Tyler, Sarah Waters and Sebastian Faulks. As for YA writers – I learned a lot from Kate Cann's novels about creating a strong voice for teen characters, a lot about economy of writing from Jacqueline Wilson and a lot about plotting from Anthony Horowitz. But there are many other writers that I love and masses of great books out there right now.

What is your fave book of all time?

Sorry, there's no way I can pick just one! All of Jane Austen's novels are up there. Plus *The Secret History* by Donna Tartt, which I've re-read several times.

What kind of music do you like?

I listen to music a lot when I write – all sorts of stuff depending on my mood and the mood of the character/scene I'm writing.

Do you have kids? Do they like your books?

I have one son, called Joe. He does like my books – though I suspect he likes football more!

ABOUT THE AUTHOR

SOPHIE MCKENZIE was born and brought up in London, where she still lives with her teenage son. She has worked as a journalist and a magazine editor, and now writes full time. Her debut was the multi-award winning *Girl, Missing* (2006), which won the Red House Book Award and the Richard and Judy Best Children's Book for 12+, amongst others. She is also the author of *Blood Ties* and its sequel, *Blood Ransom*, *The Medusa Project* series, and the *Luke and Eve* trilogy. She has tallied up numerous award wins and has twice been longlisted for the Carnegie Medal.

@ sophiemckenzie_

www.facebook.com/sophiemckenzieauthor

www.sophiemckenziebooks.com